TRIUMPHANT RETURN

Triumphant Return

LEFT BEHIND
>THE KIDS<

Jerry B. Jenkins

Tim LaHaye

WITH CHRIS FABRY

TYNDALE HOUSE PUBLISHERS, INC.
WHEATON, ILLINOIS

Visit Tyndale's exciting Web site at www.tyndale.com

Discover the latest Left Behind news at www.leftbehind.com

Published in association with the literary agency of Alive Communications, Inc., 7680 Goddard Street, Suite 200, Colorado Springs, CO 80920.

Edited by Lorie Popp

ISBN 0-8423-8350-6, mass paper

Printed in the United States of America

09 08 07 06 05
8   7   6   5   4   3   2

*To the faithful readers
of Left Behind: The Kids*

*May you live with abandon
for Jesus Christ and spread his love
and hope to those around you.*

TABLE OF CONTENTS

About the Authors

THE YOUNG TRIBULATION FORCE

Original members—Vicki Byrne Thompson, Judd Thompson, Lionel Washington

Other members—Mark, Conrad, Darrion, Janie, Charlie, Shelly, Melinda

OTHER BELIEVERS

Chang Wong—Chinese teenager working in Petra

Tsion Ben-Judah—Jewish scholar who writes about prophecy

Colin and Becky Dial—Wisconsin couple

Sam Goldberg—Jewish teenager, Lionel's good friend

Mr. Mitchell Stein—Jewish friend of the Young Trib Force

Naomi Tiberius—computer whiz living in Petra

Chaim Rosenzweig—famous Israeli scientist

Zeke Zuckermandel—disguise specialist for the Tribulation Force

UNBELIEVERS

Nicolae Carpathia—leader of the Global Community

Leon Fortunato—Carpathia's right-hand man

What's Gone On Before

JUDD and Vicki Thompson are living the adventure of a lifetime. After their wedding in Petra, the two hear of a crisis brewing in Wisconsin. Lionel Washington and Chang Wong work together to alert their friends that the GC is nearby.

After a heated debate in Wisconsin, Mark Eisman separates from his friends and heads south. He immediately encounters GC Peacekeepers led by Commander Kruno Fulcire. After returning to help the others escape, Mark is captured by the GC, and an angel encourages him to speak to others about God. Mark must finally face the guillotine with men who now believe the truth.

Judd and the rest of the Young Tribulation Force are saddened by the news about Mark, but with only a few months before the Battle of Armageddon, there is much to do. He and Vicki make contact with believers in Jerusalem who are helping defend the Old City.

Judd's friend Westin Jakes helps them travel to Jerusalem to aid rebels in the upcoming battle.

Join the Young Tribulation Force as they witness Armageddon and anticipate the return of the King of kings.

ONE

The Growing Threat

VICKI held tightly to Judd as the Global Community's Unity Army rumbled through the streets of Jerusalem. She hoped they were simply putting their tanks and soldiers into place, but Carpathia's army could attack at any moment.

Vicki had felt a sense of adventure coming to the Old City. Jamal and Lina, Judd's friends from a previous trip to Israel, had taken them in. They had also met an old man named Shivte and his wife. These rebels were trying to hold off the GC army—something Vicki believed was part of biblical prophecy.

But the closer the GC army came and the more the walls of the underground tunnel shook, the less excited she became about being here. They could have stayed in Petra.

Instead, they were in the crosshairs of the GC.

Vicki reminded herself that Jesus would soon be back to wipe out this army. And she and Judd had been overwhelmed when thousands had become believers earlier near the Temple Mount. Rabbi Tsion Ben-Judah had given the message of Jesus. Still, the thundering army sent a shiver through her.

Judd scurried to talk with one of their leaders and came back a few minutes later. "He thinks we won't see action until morning. He wants us to get some rest. Let's head back to Jamal's place."

They took a tunnel heading east, passing rebels armed with Uzis and hand grenades. Vicki had become as familiar with these tunnels over the past few months as she had with their hideout in Wisconsin. Secret passageways snaked underneath streets and buildings. Lights clanked on the stone walls as GC tanks and transport trucks rolled overhead.

A few believers spoke with rebels about Jesus when they passed, trying to convince them of the truth, but many fighters didn't want to hear about the gospel.

"We don't want your blasphemy!" one rebel yelled at a believer. "Stay away from us!"

Judd peeked through the tunnel opening and motioned Vicki forward.

By the time they made it safely to Jamal's apartment, darkness had fallen. Neither Jamal nor Lina was home. While Judd checked the computer for the latest troop movement news, Vicki pulled the curtain back on the window. "You don't have to check the computer—look out the window," she said.

They were high enough to see outside the walls of the Old City. Tanks and large vehicles were in place. Streetlights cast eerie shadows on the monstrous army.

"Our people are going up against *that*?" Judd said.

"It's not just our people—God's fighting against the army," Vicki said.

"What does Tsion say about Jerusalem? Doesn't the Bible predict it's going to fall?"

Vicki nodded and closed the curtain. "Chang said in his last e-mail that Tsion was coming here to help bring his fellow Jews into the kingdom before it was too late. Tsion believes the Unity Army will capture many rebels and conquer Jerusalem."

"Are you scared?"

Vicki hugged Judd. "I keep remembering what you said about sticking together no matter what. And if we're attacked by the GC, at least we'll die together."

"I'd rather be alive to see Jesus when he comes back, but you're right. From here on out, we stick close."

Lionel Washington sat on his bed in Petra, scanning the list of names in his prayer diary. Many of them were highlighted in yellow and had the word *home* written after their name. Ryan Daley. Pete Davidson. Mark Eisman. Chloe Williams. *It won't be long until I see all of these people,* he thought.

He wasn't as sure about his other friends on the list. Rayford Steele. Buck Williams. Tsion Ben-Judah. Lionel knew from Chang Wong that Buck and Tsion were in Jerusalem. And Rayford Steele had returned to Petra in a chopper and was probably spending time with his grandson, Kenny. But what would happen in the morning? Would Jesus come back before the GC attacked? Already the Unity Army had Petra surrounded.

What if Tsion is wrong about Petra? What if Jerusalem stands and Petra falls?

Lionel pushed the questions from his mind and prayed over each name. It had been more than seven years since the disappearances and the moment he had finally cried out to God. He had come far in those seven years, and now he was near the end.

Lionel didn't know the exact time of Jesus' return, but surely it would happen in the next day or two. What that moment would be like was anyone's guess, and Lionel couldn't wait.

Zeke called him on the radio. The burly man had asked Lionel to be part of a team that gathered weapons, ammunition, and even uniforms from fallen GC troops. "I'm out here taking a look at the edge of the camp. You should see this."

"When do you want me down there?" Lionel said.

"Before daybreak, unless the attack comes earlier, which I don't think will happen. Get a little sleep. Then head out."

Lionel had felt left out of some of the best assignments since coming to Petra and was glad Zeke had included him in this one. Now that he was close to actually going to the front line, Lionel felt unsure. Would God protect them?

He lay back on his bed and tried to fall asleep by thinking of all the people he had met in the past seven years. Carl Meninger came to mind. What a great story he had— becoming a believer while working for the

Global Community. Carl was now a vital part of the Tribulation Force in South Carolina and had seen hundreds of people believe the truth about God since Lionel and Judd had last seen him.

Lionel recalled others. Conrad Graham and Darrion Stahley, who were in Illinois, awaiting the return of Jesus with a group of inner-city believers. The stories they sent via e-mail were exciting and a little scary.

Lionel and the others had grieved the loss of the Young Trib Force Web site to the Global Community, but Chang Wong had worked his magic and was able to automatically direct anyone who logged on to Tsion Ben-Judah's Web site to a section run by the kids.

Kids, Lionel thought. *We haven't been kids since this whole thing started.* The disappearances had forced them to grow up fast.

Lionel tossed and turned on his cot for more than an hour.

Finally, he got up, dressed, and went to find Zeke.

Conrad Graham watched the sun move toward the horizon from a basement window of an abandoned house in Palos Hills, Illinois. He and the other members of the

Wisconsin group had finally settled into several homes near Enoch Dumas, the shepherd of a growing group of Christ followers from many different backgrounds. Enoch spoke with a Spanish accent, which Conrad loved. One night a Latino woman who had lived in an abandoned laser-tag park told her story. The next night it was an African-American man who admitted to everything from grave robbing to murder. Kids from the street and drug addicts all had stories of how God had reached out to them.

Conrad had been able to stay with Enoch himself and considered it as big a privilege as being in Petra. They had the chance to bring people to God every day. Though many had cautioned them to be more careful, Enoch and his followers wouldn't pass up a chance to help people receive Christ.

Conrad's mattress lay in Enoch's musty basement. The past few nights had been cold, so Conrad had given his best blanket to Shelly, who lived about three blocks away. It was shortly after Mark's death that Shelly and Conrad had renewed their friendship. Something Mark had said to Shelly caused her to give Conrad another chance after a bad disagreement in Wisconsin. They weren't going to get married anytime soon, but the fact that they could be friends gave Conrad hope.

"Don't suppose we'll get much shut-eye tonight, eh?" Enoch said, walking into the room.

"I've waited years for this," Conrad said. "No way I'm going to sleep through it."

Enoch nodded. "I know what you mean. But I don't think it'll happen until morning."

"Why is that? Doesn't the Bible say no one knows when Christ will return?"

"True. But eight in the morning our time will be the seven-year anniversary of the signing of the treaty between Carpathia and Israel. To the minute."

Enoch's love of the Bible was contagious. Since coming to the group, Conrad found himself reading more, taking notes, and seeing the Bible come alive in new ways.

"You think it's going to happen at eight tomorrow morning?" Conrad said.

"Don't know for sure, but it's as good a guess as anyone's."

Enoch flipped on a small radio and tuned to the latest news. New Babylon, the gleaming jewel of Nicolae Carpathia, had been wiped out in less than an hour. Though the GC had tried to put a positive spin on the worldwide chaos, Conrad knew from reading e-mails from Chang Wong in Petra that there were more suicides now than ever before.

The news reporter quickly turned to the Middle East where Nicolae Carpathia readied his troops. A vast army was nearing Jerusalem and had spread across the nearby desert to Petra. "An almost innumerable legion of tanks, artillery, and soldiers has assembled here to wage what should be a very quick end to a pesky enemy."

The reporter played a clip of Carpathia giving orders. It was clear that Carpathia wanted to level Petra and overrun Jerusalem.

"The only logical response to such an overwhelming military campaign is surrender," the reporter said, "but no one who has studied the history of the Judah-ites and Israelis over the last seven years believes that will happen."

"The one who should be surrendering is Carpathia," Enoch said. "God's going to make that clear real soon."

"I can't wait," Conrad said.

Judd found sleep impossible and stayed up watching the GC troops. He heard Vicki's breathing from the other room and was grateful she was getting some rest.

Judd felt concerned for Jamal and Lina, wondering what had happened to them. The last he had seen them, they were trying to convince several Israelis about Jesus.

At nearly 3 a.m. they crept inside, surprised to see Judd awake. "You won't believe who we saw at Shivte's home," Lina said, wide-eyed. "Tsion Ben-Judah. He was there with an American—"

"Buck Williams?" Judd said. He had seen the two together earlier at the Temple Mount.

"Yes! To see the teacher in person was such an honor," Lina said.

"And to see his commitment to the fight is even better," Jamal said. "He is not just here to give us moral support. He has a gun and is ready to use it."

Lina smiled and shook her fists like a child. "But we haven't told you the best news. Shivte and his sons were at the Wailing Wall this evening. They heard Dr. Ben-Judah and have believed in Messiah! All that praying we did for them, and now they are true believers."

It was all Judd could do not to rush to Shivte's house to see Buck and Tsion, but he didn't want to wake Vicki and there was no way he was going to leave without her.

When Lina left the room, Jamal spoke softly. "Shivte's sons told me they believe the

GC will come from the northwest and try to get through the Damascus Gate. We'll leave for there within the hour."

"Couldn't the GC come through just about any gate?" Judd said.

"Perhaps, but the Damascus Gate is where they need us most. I think you should leave your wife here and come with me."

Judd shook his head. "No, we've both promised—"

"This is no place for women. There will be much bloodshed. The GC is bent upon the destruction of every rebel living here in the Old City."

"Vicki and I feel God has brought us here for a reason," Judd said. "I can't leave her behind."

Jamal patted Judd's shoulder. "I understand, and I wish you success. When my wife returns, don't tell her where I've gone. Come to the Damascus Gate as soon as possible." He slipped out the door.

Jamal was gone a few moments when Lina returned with a sackful of supplies. She looked at Judd, then at the door, and burst into tears. "Tell me where he's gone! I've lost a son and a daughter to the GC! I will be with my husband at this critical hour."

"She's right," Vicki said, walking into the room.

Judd nodded. "Let's get our things. We're going to the Damascus Gate."

TWO

Bloodshed

JUDD ducked the first time he heard gunfire.
It took only a few minutes to get used to the
automatic weapons and the screams of those
who had been hit. He and Vicki, along
with their friend Lina, rushed to the end
of a tunnel near the Damascus Gate and
watched.

Rebels ran everywhere, shouting news
of the battle. The Yad Vashem Historical
Museum to the Holocaust victims had been
destroyed. Hebrew University, the Jewish
National Library, and Israel Museum were on
fire. Unity Army troops were close, and many
rebels were either dead or captured.

Are these rumors or facts? Judd thought.

Vicki clung to him tightly as they came
upon open ammunition boxes. Judd pushed
the empty boxes away and handed ammo to

Vicki as a runner hurried by. Rebels poured into the underground.

"Have you seen my husband?" Lina said to the runner.

The man ignored her, yelling instructions to other rebels.

Jamal raced inside and saw his wife. He gave Judd an icy stare. Before Judd could explain, Jamal grabbed his arm. "We're holding here. But the Dung Gate is under attack. Go."

Judd knew the Dung Gate was to the south. What the Unity Army had planned, he couldn't guess. Were they going for the Temple Mount? Would Carpathia try to set up his headquarters in that holy place?

Another report came—the Unity Army was trying to break through the Wailing Wall!

Judd glanced at Vicki, who strained under the weight of the bullets and grenades she carried. "You ready for this?" he said.

Vicki bit her lip and nodded.

Lionel looked out at the desert in the pre-dawn light. The sand had transformed into miles and miles of soldiers, horses, and weaponry. At least 200,000 troops on horse-back were in position.

He found Zeke holding a strange-looking weapon and listening for radio contact from their leader.

"What's with the horses?" Lionel said. "All those tanks and advanced weapons and they put cavalry in front?"

"Doesn't make a lick of sense to me, but I'm glad they did it," Zeke said. "We're gonna try to spook some of the horses and riders with these babies—" he patted his weapon—"and see if we can't stir things up."

"What is that?"

"It's called a DEW, short for directed energy weapon. Sends out a beam of energy that burns like fire."

Lionel winced. "I've seen one, but not that big. Can it reach the troops from here?"

"You bet," Zeke said. "We've also got fifty-calibers along the perimeter. Those will cause more damage, but they're still nothing compared to what the GC has."

A helicopter rose in the distance, and Zeke said it was Rayford Steele scouting the area. Suddenly a flash of light and a smoky cloud billowed from the Unity Army.

"We've got incoming," someone said on Zeke's radio.

"That missile's headed straight for Rayford," Zeke muttered.

As soon as Judd and Vicki arrived at the Dung Gate, another fight broke out, so they followed a group of rebels heading north. Like waves on an angry sea they surged forward, and finally Judd said they should abandon the tunnels. Judd tried to check in with Jamal by phone but couldn't get through.

Several rebels hooted and threw fists into the air as they passed on the street.

"Where are you going?" Judd yelled.

"Herod's Gate!" one said, his eyes flashing with anger.

"Judd, those men don't have the mark of the believer," Vicki said. "If they're gunned down, that's the end for them."

"I know," Judd said, "but there's no way they'll stop to listen now."

Hundreds of rebels moved toward Herod's Gate. Judd was out of breath when Vicki caught his arm. "I have an idea," she said, sprinting to the side as gunfire erupted.

What in the world is she thinking? Judd thought.

Lionel closed his eyes and said a quick prayer. Rayford Steele had made it through seven years of plagues and now this. Zeke whooped and Lionel opened his eyes. "What happened?"

"Missile went right through the chopper and came out the other side," Zeke yelled, laughing. "Looks like they might have hit some of their own troops. How do you like that? God's letting the GC take themselves out of this war."

An order came to open fire with the DEWs, and Zeke aimed his weapon. Lionel picked up binoculars and watched the perfect line of horses fall apart. Horses galloped in all directions, some knocking each other to the ground.

"Yahoo!" Zeke hollered. "Look at 'em go!"

Vicki knelt by a wounded soldier who had been shot in the leg. Judd dropped his ammo and tied a tourniquet above the wound.

A few years earlier, God had caused a cross to form on believers' foreheads, a supernatural sign that they were true followers of Christ. This man had neither the mark of Carpathia nor the mark of God.

"Take my weapon," the man groaned. "They need more fighters."

"We want to help you," Vicki said. "The Global Community is going to be defeated by God's power—"

"Leave me alone!" the man screamed, using his gun to help him stand. "I have to get back to my brothers!"

Vicki and Judd tried to stop him, but the man limped off with the crowd. Her heart ached for him and the others fighting against the overwhelming army.

Someone put a hand on her shoulder and she turned. A man carrying a gun stood behind her.

"Dr. Ben-Judah!" Vicki gasped.

"No time to talk," Tsion said, out of breath. It was strange seeing the teacher in battle dress, carrying a gun. "Keep reaching out—many still need to hear the message."

"No one wants to listen," Vicki said, but Tsion was already gone, pushed along by the crowd.

A man grabbed Tsion by the shoulders and yelled, "Hail to Ben-Judah, fearless leader of the remnant!" Another man raised Tsion off the ground and soon he was on their shoulders, people shouting his praises. As the crowd rounded the corner, Tsion was above their heads, bobbing like a parade balloon.

"This is crazy," Judd said over the noise.

"This is great," Vicki said.

They moved forward, looking for more wounded. A short time later shots fired down the street as the Unity Army came over Herod's Gate. Judd raced a few yards ahead, then came back to report that the rebels had fallen and were retreating. Judd and Vicki ducked into a doorway.

"You think Dr. Ben-Judah will be protected?" Judd said.

"I hope so," Vicki said.

"We've got to get out of here before the Unity Army comes," Judd said.

They slipped into the street and ran with the crowd.

Judd found an entrance to the tunnels and plunged down with others searching for ammunition or a place to hide. Some younger soldiers cowered in a corner, shaking and whimpering.

A man with the mark of the believer walked up to Judd and Vicki. He was armed with an Uzi and had a string of grenades strapped around his belt. "Any news of Messiah?"

"Not yet," Judd said, "but he's coming."

A Jewish woman in her twenties wiped

tears from her eyes. She wore fatigues and black boots and reminded Judd of Nada, Jamal's daughter.

"Why are you talking about legends at a time like this?" the woman said. She did not have the mark of the believer.

Vicki approached her. "Surely you've heard that a Messiah is coming."

"Yes, I've heard that all my life, but I've always thought it was a myth created by people who didn't want to deal with reality. And reality now is that we're all going to die. A fairy tale is not going to change that."

"It's no fairy tale," Vicki said, "any more than the disappearances and the earthquake and everything else that's happened during the past seven years. Jesus is coming back—at any moment—and you need to be ready."

"I'm ready to die for my country. I want to rid the earth of Nicolae Carpathia, but I won't turn my back on my religion. Get away from me."

"Please, just listen to—"

"Go!"

Judd felt bad for Vicki and even worse for the woman who seemed closed to the truth.

Another rebel nearby waved a hand, so Vicki and Judd walked over. "I heard what you said," the young man said. "And I heard

Dr. Ben-Judah last night. I almost prayed, but I was with my father and he cursed the man."

"We can help you," Judd said. "What do you need to know?"

The man looked around the darkened hallway. Several people listened. "I always thought the talk about Jesus was blasphemy. A story made up to make people hate Jews. Now I think I might have been wrong. I've been wondering if he could be the Messiah."

"We all rejected him," Judd said. "Everyone who's living now missed him. But the good news is you can be forgiven."

Judd and Vicki shared Bible verses showing that Jesus fulfilled Old Testament prophecies. Some in the hallway scoffed and kept going, but others stayed.

"Paul was a famous Jewish person from the first century," Judd said. "He studied under the best teachers and even persecuted followers of Jesus. Then something happened and this is what he wrote."

Judd held out a small Bible for the man. He read aloud, " 'I am not ashamed of this Good News about Christ. It is the power of God at work, saving everyone who believes— Jews first and also Gentiles.' "

Judd flipped a few pages and read from Romans chapter 15. " 'Remember that Christ

came as a servant to the Jews to show that
God is true to the promises he made to their
ancestors.' Jesus came and fulfilled everything predicted about him—that he would
suffer and die a cruel death, that he would
save his people, that he would—"

"But what about the verses that say
Messiah will be a king," the young rebel said,
"a ruler of the people who will establish righ-
teousness?"

Vicki smiled. "Jesus is a descendent of King
David. He is going to sit on David's throne,
just like the prophecies said. And he's going
to do it when he returns to conquer Satan
and those who serve him."

"It seems so . . . foreign to me," the man
said.

"There's a verse in Corinthians that says
we can't find God through human wisdom,"
Vicki said. "That God used the cross and the
foolishness of preaching to draw people to
himself. And that's what we're saying to you,
as foolish as it might sound. Jesus died so
your sins could be forgiven. He gave his life
and paid the penalty so you could be a true
child of God. And he offers you the chance
to believe in him right now."

"We believe Jesus could come back any
second," Judd said. He looked around at the
others who had gathered. "Don't wait any

longer to give your lives to him and serve him."

"What do we have to do?" a man said.

Judd nodded at Vicki and she understood. "Pray with me," she said. "Give your lives to God right now."

Judd glanced around the tunnel and saw several people bow their heads.

"Dear God, I'm sorry for rejecting you and the Son you sent to die for me. I do believe that Jesus is the Messiah and that he gave himself for me on the cross. I believe he rose again and made a way for me to spend eternity with you. I ask you right now to come into my life, forgive me, and make me a new person. Show me what you want me to do before Jesus returns. In his name I pray. Amen."

The people looked up as a new group of rebels ran through the tunnel. The rebel Vicki had first spoken with stood.

"What's that on your forehead?" a man said.

"You have something on yours too," the young rebel said.

Judd looked through tears at the scene. What would have happened to these people if he and Vicki hadn't come to Jerusalem? And what would happen to them now?

THREE

A Familiar Face

JUDD helped Vicki gather the new believers and prayed with them, asking God to help them spread the message of Christ's return even in the middle of the war. A few rebels ran through the tunnel passing on rumors that the Unity Army was retreating in confusion. Others said it was a trick.

"The rabbi said it is true," a newcomer said. "Something from Zechariah about God striking horses and riders."

"Where is the rabbi?" Judd said.

"I didn't see him. I was just told about—"

"Where do you *think* he is?" Judd interrupted.

"Someone said he was near Herod's Gate, but don't go unless you want to hear more about Messiah."

Judd grabbed Vicki's arm, and they

climbed out of the tunnel into the street. The silence was eerie. No gunfire, no hum of GC vehicles or crash of battering rams against gates.

As they ran for Herod's Gate, the unmistakable voice of Nicolae Carpathia blasted over a giant bullhorn. "Attention, people of Jerusalem! This is your supreme potentate!"

A crowd shouted ahead of them, and Judd and Vicki kept moving.

"Please listen, citizens," Carpathia said. "I come in peace."

More shouting.

"Come, let us reason together!" Carpathia paused. "I come to offer pardon. I am willing to compromise. I wish you no ill. If you are willing to serve me and be obedient, you shall eat the good of the land; but if you refuse and rebel, you shall be devoured by the sword. I will rid myself of my adversaries and take vengeance on my enemies. I will turn my hand against you and thoroughly purge you.

"But it does not have to be this way, citizens of the Global Community. If you will lay down your arms and welcome me into your city, I will guarantee your peace and safety."

Judd and Vicki had made it to the edge of

the crowd at Herod's Gate and looked for Tsion.

"This will be your sign to me," Carpathia said. "If at the count of three I hear silence for fifteen seconds, I will assume you are willing to accede to my requests. A single gunshot into the air during that time will be your signal that you would rather oppose me. But I warn you, half of Jerusalem is in captivity already. The entire city could be overthrown easily within an hour. The choice is yours at the count of three."

Judd wished he had a gun, but before Carpathia could even count to one, thousands of weapons fired.

When the shooting stopped, Judd noticed someone moving on a wall above the crowd. It was Tsion Ben-Judah!

"It is not too late!" Tsion said. "Make your stand for Messiah now! Repent, choose, and be saved!"

As Tsion spoke, the mark of the true believer appeared on forehead after forehead. Even at this late hour, God was working in people's hearts.

Judd looked at Vicki, who stared at the scene, fascinated. Suddenly Judd felt they should get to safety. Was it God telling him or his own fears? He wasn't about to take a chance, so he pulled her away from the gathering and to the entrance of another tunnel.

Lionel watched Unity Army riders get their horses under control. The vast army had moved toward Petra like an endless swarm of bees and had overcome whatever had spooked the horses.

Sam Goldberg scrambled up an incline toward Lionel and knelt beside him. "You ready for this?"

"How can I be?" Lionel said. "This is David versus Goliath times a million."

"Yeah, but you know who won that fight." Sam shook his head. "I'm not sure why we're out here, though. Can you imagine going into the middle of that army and trying to bring back anything?"

The order came for another round of DEWs, which Sam called ray guns. The Unity Army's front line fell back, and troops shifted and rippled like a human ocean. Lionel wondered if the GC would respond with an attack, but nothing came.

"Where's Mr. Stein?" Lionel said.

"Praying with some of the elders," Sam said. "He's upset he couldn't be in Jerusalem."

"I know how he feels."

"What, this isn't enough excitement for you?"

Judd sat by Vicki, listening to the battle above them and wondering if he had been wrong about not fighting with these brave men and women. After all, Jesus was coming back any minute—or at least within the next day. He was as sure of that as the mark on his forehead.

Sitting in the tunnel near a stairwell, it was all he could do to resist grabbing a rifle and heading up. But his promise to Vicki meant that if he went to the fight, she would have to go as well, and Judd didn't want that.

Finally the noise died a little and Vicki spoke. "I think we should go up. Maybe there are people who need more ammo or need to hear the message."

Judd nodded. "Okay, stay here and I'll check it out."

He flew up the stairs and carefully opened the door. The sight turned his stomach. Weapons and bodies of rebels littered the street. He inched out and closed the door to see if the Unity Army was near.

A *kerthunk* sounded some distance away, and Judd instinctively ducked. A shell struck the building behind him, sending debris flying. He stayed on the ground, coughing and waving a hand.

When the dust cleared, he saw a hole the size of a small car in the wall behind him.

The hole was right next to the stairwell.

"Vicki!" Judd screamed.

Lionel took a walk along the edge of the Petra defensive line, passing a man holding a DEW in one hand and a small television in the other. Lionel stopped and squinted at the screen.

"You want to see?" the man said, holding the screen higher.

Lionel thanked him and sat.

"This is a GCNN report about the war," the man said. The screen showed an aerial view of the One World Unity Army shot before sundown. The reporter explained that one-third of Carpathia's forces had surrounded Petra and that rebel leader Tsion Ben-Judah was hiding there.

"They don't have a clue," Lionel muttered.

"The other two-thirds of the Unity Army is poised to overtake the city of Jerusalem," the reporter said. "Potentate Carpathia himself reports that nearly half the city has been occupied and that it is just a matter of time before the Old City is overrun."

The report switched to a press conference with Carpathia recorded earlier. "We are confident that these are the last two rebel enclaves in the world," he said, "and that once they have been thoroughly defeated and our enemies scattered, we will realize what we have so long dreamed of: an entire world of peace and harmony. There is no place in a true global community for rebellion. If our government was anything but benevolent or did not have the attitude of 'citizen first,' there might be cause for dissention. But all we have ever attempted to do was create a utopia for society.

"It is most unfortunate that it comes to this, that we have to resort to bloodshed to achieve our goals. But we will do what we have to do."

A reporter asked about the huge army fighting against so few.

Carpathia said no effort in the cause of world peace was wasted. Then he chuckled when another reporter asked if the GC was afraid of the rebels' God.

"I do not worry about fairy tales," Carpathia answered, "but even if they did have supernatural help, they would be no match for our fighting machine. . . ."

Lionel gritted his teeth. "You're going down, Nicolae."

"Why not win this war all at once?" a reporter said. "What's the delay?"

"I am a man of peace. I always believe first in diplomacy and negotiation. The window of opportunity for settling this peacefully is always open. I had hoped that the enemies of peace would be persuaded by our size and would come to the bargaining table. But our patience is running out. They seem markedly uninterested in any reasonable solution, and we are prepared to use any means necessary. So it is just a matter of time now."

Lionel thanked the rebel for letting him watch and asked Zeke if he could spare him for a few minutes. Lionel wanted to see the reaction of the remnant.

Judd didn't care if the Unity Army was coming—he had to get to Vicki. The door to the stairwell was blocked by stones, so he went through the hole opened by the shell. He checked the street and saw a few rebels but no GC. *Must have been a stray shot*, he thought.

It was hard to breathe inside. He called for Vicki, but there was no answer. Finding the way blocked, he dashed back outside and yelled at a few passing rebels. "My wife is trapped! Can you help me?"

"I'm headed to Herod's Gate," one said. "Can't stop."

"Please," Judd said. "It'll only take a minute."

"In another minute the Unity Army might be over the wall!" The men ran on.

Finally, Judd saw a believer, and the husky man helped Judd move debris in front of the door. When they had cleared it, Judd tried the doorknob but it wouldn't open.

"Stand back," the man said. He raised his gun and blew the knob to pieces. Judd pried the door open and turned to thank the man, but he was already running away. "I hope you find your wife," he called, raising a fist. "I'll see you after Messiah comes."

Judd raced through the dust to the bottom of the steps. The tunnel wasn't as damaged as the wall outside, but there were still huge stones on the floor.

"Over here," Vicki said, coughing. She lay on the floor with a stone on her leg. "I tried to move it."

Judd's heart beat furiously as he struggled to free Vicki. The stone wouldn't budge. He snagged a gun propped against the wall and used it to pry the stone up a few inches, but Vicki's leg was still pinned. He was afraid the stone would fall and injure her worse if he tipped it farther. His arms ached as he yelled for help.

A young rebel came toward them from the other side of the tunnel. He put his gun under the stone, and together he and Judd lifted it enough for Vicki to scoot out. The stone crashed to the floor with a tremendous *thud!*

"Thank you," Vicki said, holding her leg.

Kneeling, the young man took out a knife, slit Vicki's pant leg at the bottom, and tore it until he reached her kneecap. Judd gasped at the gash in her leg. The wound was to the bone, and blood gushed out.

The young man unzipped a pocket on his jacket and pulled out some gauze and anti-septic. He poured it on the wound, and Vicki yelped in pain. When he had wrapped her leg, he said, "It doesn't look like it's broken, but someone should look at it soon."

"I'll take her to our friend's apartment right now," Judd said.

"You don't believe in Messiah," Vicki said, putting a hand on the man's arm.

The young man frowned. "Judah-ites," he muttered.

"Jesus is coming soon. You need to be ready."

"The Unity Army is coming sooner," the man said, grabbing his gun and racing up the stairs.

Judd picked Vicki up and climbed the stairs. "We'll make it to Jamal's place quicker through the street than the tunnel."

He struggled up the last steps, then was outside. Vicki buried her head in his chest as they passed rebel bodies. The sun was high in the sky now.

"How does it feel?" Judd said, looking at the bloody bandage.

"I'm okay. It's just throbbing."

"We'll get some medicine back at—" Judd stopped in the street and stared.

"What's wrong?" Vicki said.

"Over there, the guy at the edge of the curb. Is that . . . ?"

"Judd, it is! Oh, Judd, it's Tsion!"

Judd walked over to the body and put Vicki down gently. Tsion's eyes were closed, his hands together at the waist. Someone had smoothed his hair and closed his jacket over a chest wound.

Vicki wept softly, saying the man's name over and over.

"Vick, we have to go. Someone's coming."

Several rebels passed. One slowed and studied the body. "Is that who I think it is?"

Judd nodded. "The rabbi."

The man yelled at his friends, who returned. "This is our leader. We must take him."

"Take him where?" another said.

"Anywhere but here. If the Unity Army finds him, they'll give the body to Carpathia."

"We'll build a shrine for him!" another said.

"No," Judd said, "he wouldn't want that."

But two of them picked up Tsion's body and hustled down the street.

Judd gathered Vicki in his arms and neared Herod's Gate.

"They're coming!" someone shouted. Then a terrific explosion rocked the area. Judd ran the other way, looking for an escape.

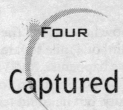

FOUR

Captured

LIONEL glanced at his sweat-soaked watch. It was a little after one in the afternoon, and the sun had heated the desert up past one hundred degrees. Shells had fallen on Petra in the past few minutes, and though Lionel hadn't seen anyone killed or injured, the bombs had landed. Had God lifted his protection?

The million-plus inside Petra were clearly antsy as they streamed toward the meeting place. Lionel saw Mr. Stein and asked what was happening.

"Dr. Rosenzweig is about to speak," Mr. Stein said.

Judd had gotten turned around by the advancing Unity Army and ended up on a street he didn't recognize. All this time in Jerusalem, planning and memorizing its layout, and now he was lost. The Old City was only a third of a mile square. This shouldn't have happened. And Vicki was losing lots of blood. She hadn't complained about her injury, but he could tell she was in pain.

She lifted her head from his shoulder, and her red hair fell across her face. "How much farther?"

Judd couldn't help thinking how beautiful Vicki was. Before the disappearances he had been attracted to girls who wore all the right clothes. Vicki had told him the only pair of designer jeans she ever owned had been bought at the thrift store near her trailer. Vicki's inner beauty shone through now, and he couldn't imagine anyone more attractive.

"Almost there," Judd assured her, though he had no idea where they were. He stopped in a doorway and gently placed her in the shadows to catch his breath and get his bearings. "I'll be right back."

She caught his arm. "Don't leave."

"Just going to make sure there's nobody around that corner. Hang tough."

Judd raced to the end of the street, flexing his arms and stretching his back. Vicki was light, but his arms felt like Jell-O after carrying her for so many blocks.

He reached the end of the street and

sneaked a peek around the corner. He recognized a storefront café half a block away. Jamal's apartment was only three or four blocks from it. He heaved a sigh of relief and turned.

Footsteps. Boots on pavement. Someone barking orders.

Had the Unity Army come this far? Or was it the rebels? Judd rushed down a stairwell and peered over the railing. He had to get back to Vicki.

Lionel watched the huge crowd at Petra quiet for Chaim Rosenzweig. The man introduced a sermon given by Dr. Shadrach Meshach Lockridge. The image of the famous black preacher was projected off two white walls of smooth stone. Lionel found some shade in front of a big rock and sat. This preaching reminded him of home, especially when he and his family would visit relatives down South.

Though the sermon took his mind off the advancing army, he knew this was designed to reach unbelievers in the camp. Lionel closed his eyes and listened. Something made him want to pray for Judd and Vicki.

Judd held his breath while a platoon of rebels passed Vicki's position and headed toward him. He rushed up the steps, and a rebel aimed his gun at him.

"No, I'm with you!" Judd shouted.

The man lowered the gun and scowled as the group kept moving. "Get out of here! Unity Army's on its way."

Judd sprinted back to Vicki and gasped when he saw her limp form draped across the top step.

"What happened?" Judd whispered as he made it to her side.

Vicki opened her eyes. "Didn't know if those were ours or theirs, so I played dead."

"Good girl. You had me fooled."

"Where are we?"

"Jamal's place is not far. We're going to be okay, and pretty soon Jesus is going to come through those clouds and we're both going to see him face-to-face."

"Can't wait."

Judd pulled her right arm around his shoulder to help her stand, but before he could pick her up, more footsteps sounded behind them. There was no time to move, so Judd tried the door of the building.

Locked.

"This way!" someone yelled from the street.

Judd and Vicki huddled in the shadows, hoping it wouldn't be the Unity Army. Soon he heard their squawking radios and GC leaders giving commands.

As the troops came into view someone said, "We don't want them escaping through the Lion's Gate to the east. After the shelling starts, we'll push them north toward Herod's Gate. They've held it since yesterday, but they'll have to open it to get through and we'll have them trapped."

The platoon passed quickly without noticing Judd and Vicki. With each heartbeat, more blood oozed from Vicki's wounded leg.

"As soon as they're around the corner, we're out of here," Judd whispered.

"What time is it?" Vicki asked, her head lolling to one side.

Judd didn't want to move to see his watch. "It's after two thirty."

"Wrong. It's time for Jesus to come back."

"Amen to that," Judd said.

A bomb exploded. Gunfire erupted. Choppers filled the sky. The platoon hurried around the corner.

Judd stood, picked Vicki up, and headed for Jamal's apartment. He cast a glance at the sky and said a simple prayer: "Come, Lord Jesus."

Lionel's heart was stirred by the video of the black preacher and the response of people in Petra. He wanted to stay until the end of the message, but he wanted to be at the battle line even more.

He quickly returned to his assigned position and looked for Zeke. Sam told him Zeke was meeting with a Trib Force member. In the past half hour, the ragtag Petra army had fired their DEWs and some bigger guns at Carpathia's vast army.

"Bet those guys are hot in those black uniforms," Lionel said.

"I wonder if those tanks are air-conditioned," Sam said, smiling.

"GC casualties," someone said from ahead. He turned and looked at Lionel and Sam. "You two part of Zeke's crew?"

"Yeah," Lionel said.

"Then you're up," the man said. "Four casualties—must be scouts—straight ahead."

"Got it," Lionel said. He grabbed a couple of duffel bags and handed one to Sam. "Let's go."

While some of Zeke's crew rushed across the sand, Lionel and Sam moved cautiously. Their job was to harvest weapons, IDs, and uniforms.

Sam reached the bodies first and tugged at the uniforms. Lionel seized weapons and put them in his duffel bag, keeping a wary eye on the line of horsemen not far away.

"Judah-ite!" a Unity Army soldier yelled. "Leave those weapons or die."

Lionel stood, clutching the bag in his right hand.

"What happened to your arm?" Another soldier laughed. "Get it caught in the lies of your leader, Ben-Judah?"

Lionel stared at him. Zeke had made Lionel a new arm, but he had left it behind for this mission. He knew it was better to say nothing, but he couldn't pass up the opportunity. He remembered two verses from Matthew and began reciting them. " 'Immediately after those horrible days end, the sun will be darkened, the moon will not give light, the stars will fall from the sky, and the powers of heaven will be shaken. And then at last, the sign of the coming of the Son of Man will—' "

"Blah, blah, blah," the first soldier said. "So you think you can beat us with a few energy weapons? Is that what your God told you?

Your God is wrong. We could simply keep moving and trample all of you without even firing a shot." He leveled a gun at Lionel. "No, your God is wrong. Dead wrong."

"Don't shoot!" Sam shouted.

The soldier fired his weapon.

Judd ran as fast as he could carrying Vicki, wishing he had stayed in the tunnels. He stuck close to the buildings, moving quietly.

"Just around this corner and we'll be able to see it," he whispered, saying it as much for himself as for Vicki.

Vicki's injured leg dangled and blood dripped. Judd didn't slow as he rounded the corner. What he saw took his breath away.

Several Unity Army soldiers stood near bodies of rebels. A soldier fired a shot at Vicki and Judd, grazing a stone just above Judd's head.

"Hands up!"

"We're unarmed," Judd yelled, trying to put Vicki down carefully. "My wife was hurt in one of the blasts near—"

"Shut up!" an officer said. He motioned at another soldier, and the second man moved toward them, his weapon raised.

Vicki turned to Judd. "Go. It's your only chance."

"Shut up!" the officer repeated.

"Make it to the tunnel," Vicki whispered. "Go."

Judd pursed his lips. "We promised each other we'd stick together. I'm not leaving you now."

"They're unmarked, sir," the soldier said, circling Judd.

Vicki collapsed and Judd tried to help her, but the soldier hit him in the back of the head with the butt of his rifle. Judd nearly passed out.

"Take them to the holding area," the officer said. "If they bat an eyelash, shoot them."

Lionel heard the gunshot as he closed his eyes and flinched. He expected to be lying on the ground with a bullet hole in his chest, but the shot whizzed past him—or *through* him. He turned to see a penny-sized hole in the sand directly behind him, then glanced back at the shooter.

If that bullet landed there, how did it miss me? Lionel thought.

"Lionel, Sam, get outta there," someone said behind them. It was Zeke, standing on the crest of a dune.

The soldier fired again while Lionel and Sam turned and walked away.

"Their weapons won't do a thing here," Zeke said. "Just wastin' their ammo."

"We'll roll over you and smash you into this desert," the officer yelled.

"Yeah, I'm sure that's what you think," Zeke said, helping Lionel and Sam back to the line. "Your guy's a loser. Ours is the true Lord."

Lionel was shaking when he made it back to the line. He found a small hole in the front of his shirt and one the same size in the back.

FIVE

Live Broadcast

CONRAD Graham awoke a little after 6 a.m. in Palos Hills, Illinois, wiped the sleep from his eyes, and hit the light button on his watch. He had wanted to stay up the whole night, but fatigue had set in a little after 2 a.m. He had been praying for his friends, praying against the Unity Army of Carpathia, and praying for those who still hadn't believed in Jesus.

They'll believe soon, one way or the other, he thought.

Enoch Dumas slept on the musty mattress in the corner, and his heavy breathing filled the room. Conrad picked up the jacket he had draped over himself and quietly tiptoed upstairs. He had told Shelly he would meet her at six thirty.

As Conrad stepped into the morning chill

and darkness, he thought about his brother, Taylor. Taylor had hated everything Carpathia stood for and lost his life trying to work against the GC. However, Taylor had been killed without ever trusting God.

That fact had haunted Conrad the past few years. No matter how many people he helped understand the truth or how many people he prayed with, there was always a shadow of regret. He would never meet Taylor again, never hear his laugh or relive old times.

Shelly met Conrad at the door of the old house where she lived with several others from the Young Tribulation Force. She gave him a hug and said she hadn't slept the whole night. "Darrion and I just kept looking at the sky and asking God to come back before daybreak, but nothing's happened."

Conrad whispered what Enoch had said the night before, and they went downstairs. Several candles lit the meeting room, and Conrad smiled at the familiar people. Darrion. Ty and his sister, Tanya. Janie. Melinda.

Charlie walked into the room yawning, followed by Phoenix, who padded up to Conrad and licked his hand. "How's Mr. Enoch doing?" Charlie asked Conrad.

"Sleeping right now," Conrad said. "Before

he fell asleep he told me to remind everybody that we're meeting at the mall at eight."

"I wouldn't miss that," Charlie said.

"What time is it over there?" Melinda said.

"I think it's early afternoon in Jerusalem,"
Shelly said. "Two or three? I wonder how
Judd and Vicki are."

Darrion switched off a handheld television. "GCNN reports total victory in the Old
City, if you can believe anything they say."

"Is that where Judd and Vicki are?" Charlie
said.

Shelly put a hand on Charlie's shoulder.
"They'll be okay. Judd and Vicki know how
to take care of themselves."

Charlie sighed. "I've been praying for them
all night."

"Maybe we should do that now," Janie
said. "Everybody, grab hands."

Conrad bowed his head and thanked God
that Jesus was coming back. "Please make it
today, Lord."

Vicki cradled Judd's head in her lap as her
tears fell on his face. He had struggled to
carry her and then fell when they reached the
transport truck.

There were few believers on the truck,

mostly rebels with chalky white skin. Vicki guessed they had lived underground the past few years since Carpathia's mark had been required.

One believer had helped her scoot near Judd. "Your friend is knocked out. He should be coming around soon."

But Judd didn't awaken during the ride or when the truck reached the remains of Teddy Kollek Stadium. The GC had set up a command post there and brought many of their prisoners to the infield area. The once beautiful structure now had a gaping hole in one side where the prisoners were led. No one was in handcuffs. There were too many of them, and besides, anyone who tried to run was shot.

The believer who had helped Vicki carried her from the truck as GC soldiers dropped Judd on a grassy area. The believer placed Vicki beside Judd.

People filled the stadium infield, and the scene was like some horror movie. Those bloodied from battle stared through vacant eyes. Unity Army troops watched for any reason to shoot.

Vicki looked around the stadium, remembering the sight from Tsion Ben-Judah's televised meetings a few years earlier. Tsion had spoken to thousands of Jewish evangelists who had traveled the world spreading the message of Jesus. The two witnesses, Moishe and Eli, had walked through this very infield. And Nicolae Carpathia had made an appearance onstage. Now, like the rest of the world, Teddy Kollek Stadium was crumbling.

A uniformed man with several bars on his shoulders approached a group of soldiers who snapped to attention.

"Yes, sir, Commander Fulcire," one of the soldiers said.

Vicki focused on the commander's face. This was the same man who had chased the kids in Wisconsin and executed Mark and Natalie Bishop.

The commander had been the top dog back in the United North American States. Now, at the moment of the biggest battle in history, Fulcire was on guard duty.

Vicki felt Judd's neck for a pulse. It was there. He was still breathing. "Hang in there," she whispered, her hair touching Judd's face. "It won't be long until we see our Lord face-to-face."

Conrad and the others in the Young Trib Force gathered with Enoch's group behind the shopping mall just before eight in the morning. People listened to Enoch's teaching, looking at the sky, some frowning.

Conrad wondered whether or not it was safe for this many people to gather in broad daylight. It was true that the GC had scaled back their Peacekeepers in the area. Most had been shipped to the Middle East. But citizens loyal to Nicolae Carpathia received cash for every unmarked citizen they captured or killed, and Conrad felt antsy. When Enoch suggested they move to the inner court of the empty mall, he felt better.

Enoch took a flurry of questions from the group.

Charlie started it all by asking, "When's it gonna happen?"

Enoch said he believed today was the day, then was interrupted by a woman in the back holding a tiny TV. "Look like somebody done took over the GC's airwaves again. That Micah guy runnin' things at Petra is gonna speak about what comes next."

Darrion and some others pulled out their little TVs.

"Should we listen, Brother Enoch?" the woman said. "Will you be offended?"

"Hardly," Enoch said, taking out his own TV. "What could be better than this? Dr. Rosenzweig is a scholar's scholar. Let's have church."

"Why don't we line up the TVs on that bench and turn up the volume so everyone can hear?" Conrad said.

"Wonder what old Nicolae thinks of this broadcast," Darrion said.

Dr. Rosenzweig was just beginning when they turned up the volume. He sat at a table with a Bible open before him.

"I speak to you tonight probably for the last time before the Glorious Appearing of our Lord and Savior, Jesus Christ the Messiah," Chaim said. "He could very well come during this message, and nothing would give me greater pleasure. When he comes there will be no more need for us to fight Antichrist and his False Prophet. The work will have been done for us by the King of kings.

"But as he did not return seven years to the minute from the signing of the covenant between Antichrist and Israel, many are troubled and confused."

Chaim continued, saying he believed Jesus would return before midnight, Israel Time. Then he spoke to those who had not accepted Jesus as Messiah.

Conrad moved closer to the tiny screens when a Web site address appeared beneath Dr. Rosenzweig. Anyone making a decision for Christ was asked to let Chaim know about it.

Dr. Rosenzweig read from Matthew 24 and explained what he believed would come next. "This *is* the last day of the Tribulation that was prophesied thousands of years ago! Today is the seventh anniversary of the unholy and quickly broken covenant between Antichrist and Israel. What is next? The sun, wherever it is in the sky where you are, will cease to shine. If the moon is out where you are, it will go dark as well because it is merely a reflection of the sun. Do not fear. Do not be afraid. Do not panic. Take comfort in the truth of the Word of God and put your faith in Christ, the Messiah."

Conrad was thrilled when Chaim turned to Zechariah and read prophecy written hundreds of years before Jesus' birth.

Then the man leaned forward, looked into the camera, and spoke. "One of our first-century Jews, Peter, said, 'Anyone who calls on the name of the Lord will be saved.' I cannot choose more appropriate words than his when I speak to fellow Jews, saying, 'People of Israel, listen! God publicly endorsed Jesus of Nazareth by doing wonderful miracles, wonders, and signs through him, as you well know. But you followed God's prearranged plan. With the help of lawless

Gentiles, you nailed him to the cross and murdered him. However, God released him from the horrors of death and raised him back to life again, for death could not keep him in its grip.

" 'King David said this about him: "I know the Lord is always with me. I will not be shaken, for he is right beside me. No wonder my heart is filled with joy, and my mouth shouts his praises! My body rests in hope. For you will not leave my soul among the dead or allow your Holy One to rot in the grave. You have shown me the way of life, and you will give me wonderful joy in your presence."

" 'Dear brothers, think about this! David wasn't referring to himself when he spoke these words I have quoted, for he died and was buried, and his tomb is still here among us. But he was a prophet, and he knew God had promised with an oath that one of David's own descendants would sit on David's throne as the Messiah. David was looking into the future and predicting the Messiah's resurrection. He was saying that the Messiah would not be left among the dead and that his body would not rot in the grave.

" 'This prophecy was speaking of Jesus,

whom God raised from the dead, and we all
are witnesses of this. Now he sits on the
throne of highest honor in heaven, at God's
right hand. And the Father, as he had promised, gave him the Holy Spirit to pour out
upon us, just as you see and hear today.

" 'So let it be clearly known by everyone in
Israel that God has made this Jesus whom
you crucified to be both Lord and Messiah!'

"Beloved," Chaim raced on, "the Bible tells
us that 'Peter's words convicted them deeply,
and they said to him and to the other apostles, "Brothers, what should we do?" '

"Do you find yourself asking the same
today? I say to you as Peter said to them,
'Each of you must turn from your sins and
turn to God, and be baptized in the name of
Jesus Christ for the forgiveness of your sins.
Then you will receive the gift of the Holy
Spirit. This promise is to you and to your
children, and even to the Gentiles—all who
have been called by the Lord our God.'

"Oh, children of Israel around the globe,
I am being signaled that our enemy is close
to wresting back control of this network.
Should I be cut off, trust me, you already
know enough to put your faith in Christ as
the Messiah."

Chaim closed by reading a prophecy from

Isaiah 53 given more than seven hundred years before the birth of Christ.

Conrad wondered how many watching had responded to the man's appeal.

Six

Deadly News

Lionel watched in awe as the sun dipped toward the horizon. He had never seen such a sight. Throughout the day, the sky had been clear. Now, fluffy marshmallow-like clouds seemed to appear, one after another, moving quickly above him.

After the incident in the desert, Sam and Lionel asked Zeke for a break and Zeke agreed. Sam and Lionel moved back into camp and ate their evening meal. When Mr. Stein joined them, Sam explained all that had happened.

Mr. Stein saw the fear in Sam's eyes. "The Lord has protected us these past few years," he said, smiling. "Why would you think it would be different now?"

"We've never gone up against that before," Sam said, pointing to the vast army.

"But look at that," Mr. Stein said, gesturing to the sky. The clouds had formed a canopy above them, and the reflection of the orange sun took their breath away. "Your outlook needs an up-look. Any God who could create that masterpiece should be trusted with your life, don't you think?"

Lionel looked at the Unity Army. All day they had advanced at a snail's pace. Now the army covered the desert like the clouds covered the sky, a perfect mirror. Only one was beautiful and the other hideous.

Vicki held Judd until the fatigue stiffened her whole body. She lay down beside him, an arm draped over him. The rising and falling of his chest let her know he was still alive.

The sun's orange glow reflected in the clouds above, clouds she hadn't seen earlier. She wished Judd would wake up so they could share this.

She tried to shut out the conversation of the GC soldiers around them. Many mocked the prisoners, saying they were Jesus freaks or Ben-Judah freaks or cursing them. "I don't know why they had us take prisoners in the first place," one said. "We should have killed them all where they stood."

Later, when a group of soldiers moved toward Vicki, she propped herself up on an elbow. Her leg ached from the deep wound, and she worried it would get infected.

Commander Fulcire picked out prisoners to be taken away. He turned and waved a hand at Judd. "And that one too."

"What!?" Vicki shouted. "Why are you moving him?"

Fulcire glared at Vicki. "We're burning the dead for health reasons—"

"He's not dead!" Vicki yelled.

Fulcire cocked his head and stared at her.

"Please, God," Vicki prayed silently, "help Judd wake up."

"Do I know you?" Fulcire said, squinting.

"This is my husband," Vicki said, ignoring the question and looking away. "I won't let you take him."

Two soldiers approached Judd. "Your husband is dead, rebel," one soldier said, taking Judd's arms. The other moved to his legs and stooped.

Vicki breathed another prayer as she fell on Judd's torso and screamed in pain.

Judd's eyes fluttered and he moaned.

Fulcire moved closer as the two men tried to pick Judd up. The commander held up a hand, so the soldiers dropped Judd.

"Ah, back from the dead, are we?" Fulcire crooned. He knelt beside Vicki. "Something looks familiar about you. You're from the United North American States, right?"

Vicki hugged Judd and ignored the man. She decided she wouldn't speak again unless she had to. If this guy figured out who she was, her life was over.

Fulcire stood. "Take them both to interrogation."

Vicki didn't protest when the men helped them to their feet. Judd was still groggy, but he made eye contact with Vicki and put a hand to the back of his head.

"We're going to be okay," Vicki said. "Look at the clouds."

Judd glanced skyward, and his mouth opened in an *O*. "He should be here by now, don't you think?"

"Soon," Vicki said.

Conrad glanced at his watch. It was about noon in the Midwest, and the people asked Enoch to teach them more. Conrad listened intently and looked at the sky. Something was happening with the clouds.

Enoch explained that twenty-one judgments had come from heaven in three sets of seven. These showed God's mercy on one hand, calling people to repentance, but also God's anger at evil. According to the Bible, the judgments were poured out by angels from bowls or vials.

Enoch went through each of the seven bowls, judgments that came in the form of sores on people's bodies, the sea turning to blood, rivers and springs turning to blood, the sun becoming hot enough to burn people alive, New Babylon's darkness, and the drying up of the Euphrates River.

"The seventh bowl judgment, the one we still await, will be poured out upon the *air* so that lightning and thunder and other celestial calamities announce the greatest earthquake in history. It will be so great it will cause Jerusalem to break into three pieces in preparation for changes during Christ's millennial kingdom. It will also be accompanied by a great outpouring of hundred-pound hailstones.

"And what will the general response be from the very ones God is trying to reach and persuade? Revelation 16:21 tells us that 'they cursed God because of the hailstorm, which was a very terrible plague.'"

"And this is what's coming next?" an older man said.

"In advance of the Glorious Appearing," Enoch said. "Yes."

Conrad thought of Judd and Vicki in Jerusalem. If they were still there and still alive, the ground would soon be shaking beneath them.

Judd was dropped on his back near the Unity Army command post outside what was left of Teddy Kollek Stadium. It took him a few seconds to catch his breath. Soldiers plopped Vicki down beside him, and he tried to help her get into a comfortable position.

"Are you okay?" Vicki said.

"There's a knot on the back of my head and I have a headache the size of Cleveland, but I think I'm okay. What happened?"

Vicki filled him in. "I think Fulcire knows who I am. I mean, he may not have figured it all out, but he remembered something about me."

"Let's tell him we were over here on vacation and just happened to get caught up in the war."

"And what do we tell him about not taking Carpathia's mark?"

Judd bit the inside of his cheek. "We have a skin condition?"

Vicki shook her head. "I'm glad one of us has a sense of humor right now."

There were several other prisoners on the sidewalk outside the stadium. Some looked like they had been beaten and were waiting for another round of questioning.

Listening to the soldiers, Judd picked up information that Nicolae Carpathia was in Jerusalem but would soon be heading to Petra. Rebels currently held the Temple Mount, but the Unity Army was going after them. The GC now controlled most of the Old City. Something was brewing to the south and northeast, a revolt of some sort among Unity Army troops, but Judd couldn't figure out what that was about.

A GCNN reporter with a camera crew shuffled by taking shots of the prisoners. Judd and Vicki turned their heads as they passed.

"This is something, isn't it?" Vicki said. "To be in the middle of Carpathia's army on the last day of the world."

"If this is the last day," Judd said.

"What do you mean?"

"What if Tsion was wrong? Even Jesus said no one knows the hour when he's going to return."

"True, but I think he was talking about the

Rapture when he said that. From Daniel 9:27 we know that the Glorious Appearing happens seven years after—" Vicki stopped as Commander Fulcire returned and spoke in hushed tones to another officer.

The officer hustled to Vicki, held out a small electronic device, and mashed her fingers across a square pad.

"He knows," Vicki whispered.

The commander returned with a smile, holding the device. He turned it around, and Judd tried not to react. Vicki's picture, along with her personal information, flashed on the screen. She was one of the most wanted young people in the world.

"So, Vicki B—" Fulcire grinned—"we finally meet. Who would have thought I'd have to come all the way to Israel to find you? What a lucky break."

"Your luck is about to run out," Vicki mumbled.

"I'm sorry. What was that?" Fulcire said, kicking at Vicki's injured leg.

Judd wanted to kill Fulcire, but he scooted closer to Vicki, trying to protect her. She writhed in pain, and Judd noticed blood seeping from her bandage.

"You've been with the rebels," Fulcire said. "We've wiped out most of them, but some are still in hiding. I want to know where."

"Even if I knew, I'd never tell you," Vicki said through clenched teeth.

"That's the same thing all you Judah-ites say. That friend of yours back in the States, Mark something. He said he would never tell us a thing, but the prospect of the blade—how should I say it?—loosened his tongue."

"You monster," Vicki said.

"Mark didn't tell you anything," Judd yelled.

Fulcire glanced at Judd and smiled. He motioned for a soldier.

"What are you doing?" Vicki said.

"Maybe you won't tell us what we know if we threaten *you*, but what about this husband of yours?"

"No!" Vicki screamed.

"It's okay," Judd said, standing. "This is all going to be over soon. You and your army are going back to dust—"

A soldier hit Judd on the knee with the butt of his rifle, and Judd fell with a sickening thud. Something cracked in his leg as he tumbled to the ground.

The soldier pointed his rifle at Judd's head and looked at Fulcire.

"Do you have anything to tell us now?" Fulcire said to Vicki.

"You know where our leaders are," Vicki cried. "They're all at Petra."

"We know the rebels use tunnels," Fulcire said. "I'd rather not blow up all these buildings to find them. Lord Carpathia will need them. Show us where the rebels are."

Vicki looked at Judd. If she didn't give Fulcire the information he wanted, Judd would die. If she did give the information, rebels would die.

"Don't do it," Judd said, gasping at the pain.

The soldier hovering over Judd kicked him, and blood spurted from his mouth. Judd's head hit the concrete hard, and Vicki fell on top of him.

"They're going to kill us anyway," Judd managed to say. "Don't tell them anything."

"I won't let them hurt you," Vicki said.

The soldier raised his gun again, and Vicki held up a hand. "Stop! I'll tell you what you want, but you have to stop."

Fulcire waved the soldier away and knelt near Vicki. "I'm waiting."

"No," Judd groaned.

"I'll take you there," Vicki said.

Lionel went home and closed the door. He had been so excited about the return of Christ, but the oncoming army sent shivers down his spine every time he looked at the desert. The sun had dipped below the horizon now, and a full moon peeked out from behind the increasing clouds.

A roar rose outside and Lionel's heart fell. Had he missed the return of Jesus? No, there would be signs in the heavens—maybe that's what the clouds were!

He hurried outside to see tens of thousands gathering their evening meal applaud people riding on ATVs. Rayford Steele was being carried by someone from the Tribulation Force. Lionel had heard earlier that Rayford had been injured or possibly killed in an accident. People waved and screamed encouragement as the former pilot for Nicolae Carpathia passed.

Lionel joined several people who had gathered to pray. The Unity Army was less than a football field away from Zeke and the others at the front lines. *The battle has already been won*, Lionel thought. *God said he was going to take care of these people and either I'm going to believe it or not!*

Lionel rushed toward Rayford Steele's home. He had to talk with someone he knew. As he approached, he heard voices inside and recognized Chaim Rosenzweig's. Lionel was about to knock when a cell phone chirped.

"Yeah, Sebastian, it's Ray. . . . I'm okay, a little banged up, but okay. What's the latest on Buck? . . . No, go ahead and tell me. . . ." There was a long pause. "Does Mac know how it happened?" Another pause. "Okay, thanks for letting me know."

"Is it Buck?" Chaim said, his voice shaky.

"Yeah. Mac found his body in Jerusalem. He was torn up pretty bad."

"I cannot believe Buck and Tsion are both dead," Chaim said.

Lionel staggered away from the door. *Both dead?* He sprinted down the hillside to find Sam, praying for Judd and Vicki as he ran.

SEVEN

Lights Out

VICKI huddled close to Judd in the back of the truck as they entered a gate at the Old City. Bodies lay strewn about the road, and the truck shimmied as it rolled over dead rebels. The rebels' clothes lay torn and in some cases ripped apart, which made Vicki wonder if the GC hadn't gone through their clothing for valuables. She closed her eyes at the horrific scene.

"Vicki, you can't do this," Judd whispered. "I won't let you."

"Trust me," she said. "I won't give them anything."

"Then what are we doing?"

Vicki glanced up. The canvas canopy over the truck had been pulled back, and they could see the sky. Clouds parted, showing the full moon. "I'll think of something."

The truck ground to a halt, its brakes squealing. Vicki's leg ached with a pain she had never experienced. Judd's leg was nearly useless. She doubted he could walk.

"Out!" Commander Fulcire shouted.

A soldier on the ground helped Vicki down, but he pushed Judd off so he landed hard, crying out in pain.

"I swear if you hurt him any more, I'll tell you nothing!" Vicki yelled.

Fulcire seized Judd by an arm and pulled him up. "He's okay. Just a couple of scratches, eh, young man? Now show us an entrance, and no warning your compatriots that we're coming."

Vicki walked slowly away from the truck, looking at buildings and street signs.

"Stop here," Fulcire said. He walked around Judd and faced Vicki. "We know there are tunnels—show us or we add you to the dead."

Judd nudged Vicki and pointed up. A light shot across the night sky in front of the moon. Vicki gasped and Fulcire looked up as well.

"Guards, take him!" Fulcire said.

But as soon as they moved toward Judd, the moon went black. The streets disappeared under a dark blanket. Several soldiers screamed.

"It's just like in New Babylon," one said.

"It's another plague! And you know what happened to that city!"

"Shut up!" Fulcire ordered. "Try the truck lights."

"Come on," Vicki whispered to Judd. "Let's get out of here."

But before they could move, the lights on the truck blazed, lighting up the street. The soldiers sighed with relief.

Fulcire radioed someone and received a report from Teddy Kollek Stadium that their lights were all working and there was nothing to worry about. He turned to Judd and Vicki.

"Do you see that, Commander?" Vicki said, pointing at the sky. "That's part of the prophecy. God said the sun and moon will be dark on this day. He's going to punish the world for its evil. This is happening around the world, and you'd better get ready for the next thing he's going to do."

Scores of verses from the Old and New Testaments flooded Vicki's mind. All spoke of the wrath of God poured out on the earth. She wanted to spill the verses out one after another.

The commander smirked. "The moon goes behind a cloud and she claims it's a miracle of God."

Soldiers laughed, but not very hard, Vicki

thought. They had seen enough in the last few years to make them wary.

"We've heard your prophecies of gloom and doom," Fulcire snapped. "Show us the entrance to—"

"You may have heard enough, but obviously you haven't seen enough," Vicki shot back. Her words appeared to stun him.

"Babylon the great has fallen, just like God said it would," she continued. "And soon you will see the Son of Man coming in the clouds with great power and glory. He'll be on a white horse, and he will make war with you and will overcome you and your armies."

"Yes, Jesus will show up by and by, pie in the sky, and then we'll all die," Fulcire mocked. "But you won't be around to see him, will you, Judah-ite?" He pulled a pistol from a holster around his waist and aimed it at Judd's head. "Now point the way to one of the tunnels, or I'll send your precious husband to be with Jesus where he can ride all the white horsies."

Vicki looked at Judd, his face lit by the truck's lights. It struck her as strange that it would end this way. They had survived seven years of disasters, only to be killed a few hours—maybe a few minutes—before the return of Christ.

"I love you," Judd whispered. There didn't

seem to be a hint of fear in his voice. "I'll always love you."

"Your choice," Fulcire said, cocking the pistol.

Conrad had jumped to his feet and cried out with the others when the early afternoon sun disappeared from the sky in Palos Hills, Illinois. The temperature dropped, and the world turned pitch dark.

But it was the roaring, whistling sound that spooked everyone the most. It sounded like a jet coming in for a landing, engines screaming. Conrad looked up and saw a fiery trail behind something—maybe a spaceship, airplane, or falling star. He didn't know what it was, but he wasn't about to stay and find out. He grabbed Shelly's hand, and they ran for cover.

"Don't be afraid!" Enoch yelled. "This was prophesied. It's all part of God's plan."

The object crashed on the other side of the mall, and everyone rushed to it. Streetlights popped on as Conrad and Shelly ran, hand in hand. They found a ten-foot-wide hole in the road, smoke billowing, and heat so intense they couldn't get close.

Tom and Josey Fogarty darted across the

street, heading for safety with their little boy, Ryan.

"Here comes another one!" Ty Spivey shouted.

The falling object roared overhead. Flames licked at its edges as it plunged to earth, and people screamed. Conrad took Shelly's hand again, and they bolted toward the Fogartys.

"You can come to our house," Shelly said to Conrad.

"I believe we're protected!" Enoch yelled behind them. "None of the judgments from heaven harmed God's people! We bear his mark, his seal! He will protect us!"

But Conrad and Shelly continued to run, with the screaming meteor falling. When a terrific explosion lit the darkness, Conrad looked back. This meteor—at least twice as big as the first—slammed into one of the large stores at the mall.

"Wonder how the GC is going to spin this," Shelly said.

"They'll probably tell everybody they shouldn't be afraid," Conrad said. "After all, it's just the sky falling on them."

Lionel reached the defense perimeter of Petra as the moon darkened and GC troops lit flashlights and high-tech lanterns. When the first streaks of light crossed the sky, the Petra rebels *ooh*ed and *aah*ed. Then the first meteor fell several hundred yards from Lionel's position, and the Unity Army panicked. Horses reared and soldiers screamed orders.

The next meteor slammed into a mass of tanks and transport vehicles, causing a huge explosion. Soldiers flew into the air. The front lines of the army withdrew—how far Lionel couldn't tell.

Rocks nearby shook with the crashing of each meteor. While the Unity Army was struck again and again, Petra remained safe.

Someone turned on large searchlights near the camp and pointed them straight up. The light allowed Lionel to see the edges of the Unity Army and the clouds above that bubbled and churned like boiling macaroni. There was a flash in the distance. Then came a low rumble.

Something big was happening. Lionel felt chills. He wondered if Judd and Vicki were seeing the same thing. Or if Judd and Vicki were even alive.

Vicki covered her eyes as Commander Fulcire leveled the pistol at Judd. She heard a whooshing sound, and something approached overhead. Several men yelled and Vicki looked again, surprised to see Commander Fulcire with his gun at his side, staring into the darkened sky.

"Incoming!" someone shouted from the truck.

The soldiers hit the dirt before a fiery sphere hurtled to earth. The impact shook the ground, and Judd nearly fell down from the shock.

Radios blared, soldiers ran, and everyone seemed confused.

"What's going on?" Judd whispered.

"God's show is starting," Vicki said.

Fulcire motioned to a nearby soldier. "Get these two back in the truck!"

The soldier hustled Judd and Vicki to the back of the vehicle and told them to climb inside. Vicki tried to help Judd, but he had trouble lifting his injured leg. Judd grasped a handle on the side and tried to pull himself up, but before he could, another meteor flew overhead and the soldier hit the ground. In the confusion, darkness, and roar of the explosion, Vicki grabbed Judd's hand and pulled him to the side of the truck, out of sight. The soldier whimpered on the ground.

"Get down and crawl under," Vicki said. "They might not see us."

They scrambled underneath and watched soldiers rush for safety. But where could they go? The meteors looked like they were as big as cars, so the craters they left behind had to be huge.

"Did you know this was coming?" Judd whispered.

Vicki nodded and inched closer to the edge of the truck so she could see the sky. "In Isaiah, I think. There's also supposed to be a sign in the heavens."

"What kind of sign?"

"I don't know what form it will take, but that's supposed to happen before Jesus comes back."

"Maybe the clouds are the sign."

"Could be."

Judd pointed across the street. "You know there's an entrance to the tunnels about half a block away?"

"I wasn't going to tell them."

"You were just going to let me die?" Judd was smiling.

"That's what you said to do. And that part about loving me forever was nice."

"Everybody in the truck!" Commander Fulcire yelled. "Now!"

"Sir, the prisoners . . . they're not here!" a soldier at the back said.

The soldier tried to defend himself, but Fulcire wouldn't listen. A gun fired and the soldier fell, his face looking straight at Judd and Vicki. A red stain pooled around his body.

Vicki clamped a hand over her mouth to keep from screaming. Soon, more meteors fell, and it appeared that Fulcire was more interested in getting to safety than finding Judd and Vicki.

The soldiers piled into the truck, and Judd and Vicki rolled to their left into the darkness. The truck sped through the gate as they limped to the entrance to the tunnel. Seconds later a meteor slammed into the earth, just past the gate, shattering windows. Judd and Vicki went inside, gingerly climbing to the next floor where they could see the scene. Fulcire's truck had tried to stop before a huge crater, but it teetered on the edge. Fulcire shouted commands as he climbed out the passenger-side window.

Soldiers began jumping from the rear, in spite of Fulcire's orders. The commander made it out of the truck's cab and climbed on top. But when several more soldiers leaped out the back, the truck tipped forward. Fulcire grabbed for something to hold on to, but the truck's top was too slick. He tried to jump to a concrete walkway but didn't make it. His screams echoed as he and the truck plunged down.

Lightning flashed, casting eerie bursts of light on the Old City.

"What do you want to do?" Vicki said.

"Let's see how far we can get through the tunnels," Judd said. "Maybe we'll find someone who can help us."

"I don't want to be in here when Jesus comes," Vicki said.

"Me either, but with this busted leg, they'll catch us outside."

Vicki found Judd a place to rest. "This time let me find someone and bring them back to help," she said. "Stay right here."

EIGHT

Lightning Show

LIONEL sat with Sam on Petra's perimeter and watched God's light show. Lightning flashed through the deepening clouds, thick streaks of gold firing overhead. He remembered watching a tornado years before the Tribulation began, but that didn't compare with this.

Lightning increased, with hundreds and thousands of bolts crashing to the desert floor every second. It was like the end to a terrific fireworks display, only this one was a million times brighter and stronger. Thunder shook the ground, and Lionel tried to cover his ears.

Sam pulled out his tiny television and cupped a hand around the screen so they could see it. The Global Community News Network treated God's light show as a nonstory. Instead, their coverage focused on the war effort. Unity generals reported troops heading toward the Valley of Megiddo.

Nicolae Carpathia was shown getting onto a huge horse. "I am pleased with the reports from the South and from the Northeast. And now we are about to embark on one of our most strategic initiatives. A third of our entire fighting force will advance upon the rebel stronghold cowering in Petra. Intelligence tells us that a paltry defensive unit has rung the city round about, but they are hopelessly outnumbered and have already offered to surrender."

"Did you know we were ready to surrender?" Sam said.

Lionel shook his head. "I'm glad we're on the side of the one causing this lightning and thunder."

Carpathia answered questions, lying about his contact with leaders in Petra. "We made peaceful overtures to the leadership, offering amnesty for any who would voluntarily leave the stronghold and take the mark of loyalty. Our understanding is that many wished to make this move, only to be slaughtered by the leadership. Many will recall that it was this very leadership who assassinated me, serving only to give me the opportunity to prove my divinity by raising myself from the dead.

"Well, this time around, there will be no negotiating. Loyalists to our New World Order have either been murdered or have escaped, so intelligence tells us Petra is now inhabited solely by rebels to our cause, murderers and blasphemers who have thumbed their noses at every attempt to reason with them."

Carpathia waved a sword for the camera and continued. "I shall personally lead this effort, with the able assistance, of course, of my generals. We shall rally the troops as soon as we arrive, and the siege should take only a matter of minutes."

Carpathia raced off on the horse, and a reporter called after him, "All the best to you, holy one! And may you bless yourself and bring honor to your name with this effort!"

"Won't be long now," Lionel said.

Conrad and Shelly huddled together on the front porch of the house where Shelly was staying. Conrad had a Bible open and could read by the lightning strikes. Enoch had shown Conrad many verses about what was to come.

Conrad turned toward the end of the Old Testament to Zephaniah and read some verses to Shelly. " 'That terrible day of the Lord is near. Swiftly it comes—a day when strong men will cry bitterly.

" 'It is a day when the Lord's anger will be poured out. It is a day of terrible distress and anguish, a day of ruin and desolation, a day of darkness and gloom, of clouds, blackness, trumpet calls, and battle cries. Down go the walled cities and strongest battlements!

" 'Because you have sinned against the Lord, I will make you as helpless as a blind man searching for a path. Your blood will be poured out into the dust, and your bodies will lie there rotting on the ground.' "

He closed the Bible, and Shelly scooted closer. Houses crackled and burned not far away. The acrid, smoky smell of the meteors filled the air.

"What do you think all that means?" Shelly said.

"I guess it means your life is worthless if you fight against God," Conrad said. "He's going to win every time."

Suddenly the lightning and thunder stopped. The sky was pitch-black, and Conrad wondered how long God would wait. Soon Jesus would return—but would he be seen just in Jerusalem or everywhere?

Conrad put an arm around Shelly. "Enoch

says he's going to find a way to get to Israel as soon as possible. He's even going to try and raise money for his people to go there."

"I'd do anything to see Jesus start setting up his kingdom," Shelly said. "Let's go together."

Conrad smiled, pulling her close. "We could stay with Judd and Vicki."

Vicki limped through the deserted tunnel, listening for rebels. The pain in her leg had gotten worse, and it was difficult to walk. She tripped and fell over a dead rebel, and her wound opened again.

She found medical supplies and bandages and stumbled back to Judd. She guessed his leg was broken, so there was nothing she could do except put a blanket over him and try to make him comfortable.

When she got her own bandage off, the sight turned her stomach. The rock had torn away her skin, and the deep gash was now a sickly color. She poured in some antiseptic and thought she was going to pass out from the pain. After rebandaging the wound, she crawled up the stairs and peeked outside. The thundering of the guns had stopped. A few scattered shots were fired every now and then, but the battle seemed to be over. The GC had overtaken Jerusalem just like the Bible said.

She returned to Judd and lay down beside him. She remembered the words of her Little League coach: "Leave everything on the field."

She smiled, thinking they had done just that—they'd used all their energy to help people. Whatever happened next would happen without their help.

Lionel and Sam sat in the stillness of Petra, darkness covering the land. Rebels with weapons seemed restless, waiting for something to happen. Sam gave Lionel a canteen of water, and he took a long drink.

"Carpathia's on the move," Lionel said. "We might see him tonight."

"I'd like to see him get thrown into the lake of fire where he belongs," Sam said. "I can't wait until—" He stopped in midsentence.

Lionel had tilted his head back and taken another drink from the canteen. Suddenly a light flashed in the sky and something buzzed, like the sound of a light saber in one of those old *Star Wars* movies. Sam pointed, mouth agape, and Lionel pulled the canteen from his mouth, water spilling.

A yellow streak of light—like lightning, only it wasn't—pulsed in the sky. It started near the horizon and went straight up miles into the sky. Two-thirds of the way up, another yellow streak intersected the first one, forming a huge cross.

Lionel was so overcome he dropped the canteen. He could only imagine what was going through the minds of the Unity Army soldiers.

Conrad shielded his eyes from the blazing cross and couldn't help smiling. A warm feeling surged through his body. He and Shelly stood and stared in awe.

"He's really coming back," Shelly whispered, full of emotion. "This is the sign of the Son of Man Dr. Ben-Judah wrote about."

"Amazing," was all Conrad could say.

"Let's find Enoch," Shelly said.

On the way, Conrad stopped outside a house and peered in the front window. A huge television stood against the far wall. People inside screamed and pointed. On the screen was the yellow cross, blazing for the whole world to see.

Judd opened his eyes and noticed a glare shining through a tiny hole in the brick wall. A bomb must have exploded, he thought, and created the crack there. He glanced down and noticed Vicki on his chest.

She shifted slightly and looked up at him. "You're awake. How do you feel?"

Judd put a hand in front of his face. "Fine except for that annoying light coming from over there." He gestured at the wall. "You think the Unity Army's put up floodlights?"

"If they have, they're yellow," Vicki said. "Listen."

Judd sat up quietly, straining to hear a hum coming from outside. "It's weird that we'd hear it down—"

"Shh," she said. "Can you feel it vibrating?"

Judd listened a few more seconds. "It almost sounds like the light in the aquarium back home. Only a million times louder."

Vicki's gaze darted left and right.

"What is it?" Judd said.

"I don't know. Maybe we've missed it," Vicki said.

"Jesus?"

"Yeah, maybe he's already come back and we were down here. Or maybe . . ."

"What?"

She rolled to her knees and stood, peeking out of the crack in the wall. "There was supposed to be a sign in the sky. . . ."

"No way I'm going to miss this," Judd said, racing her up the stairs.

They plunged through the door and into the street, not caring that the GC was nearby. The sight in the sky took their breath away. Judd put an arm around Vicki and hugged her.

"A cross," she whispered. "Of course!"

Judd couldn't take his eyes from the yellow pulsing light. He wondered what was happening at the Temple Mount right now and in the desert with Carpathia's army. Could the GC sense their end was near?

"Wait a minute," Vicki said. "What are you doing? You have a broken leg and you just . . ."

Judd stared at her. "And you—we just ran up those stairs, but . . ." He put all his weight on his bad leg. No pain. He wasn't even sore. "I thought for sure it was broken."

Vicki felt the back of his head. "There was a big knot here. What happened?"

Judd's eyes grew wide as he pulled Vicki's pant leg up and unwrapped her bandage.

"What are you doing?" she said. "I want to keep it covered so it won't get infected."

"You were limping on this, right?"

"Yeah, but—"

Vicki's mouth dropped open. Her leg looked perfectly normal. No skin tears, no blood, no scars. Not even a scratch.

"We've both been healed!" Judd said.

They jumped and giggled like schoolchildren. Judd felt ten pounds lighter.

"What do we do?" Vicki said, unable to stop smiling.

"Jesus is supposed to come back to the Mount of Olives, right?"

She nodded. "And he's going to split it in two."

"Okay, there's got to be another mount close by where we can see everything."

"Mount Scopus," Vicki said.

"Mount Scopus it is," Judd said. "Let's go."

Lionel picked up the canteen and screwed on the lid as he watched the cross. It was a symbol of how far God would go to show his love.

Lionel felt pressure on his left arm, and the one Zeke had made for him pushed forward.

Sam yelled and pointed, startled by something on Lionel's clothes.

Lionel brushed his hand against his shirt,

thinking there might be an insect on him. "What is it?"

Sam stared at Lionel's left arm. Lionel raised it. His arm had returned. Two hands.

A miracle!

Lionel raised both hands toward the cross and fell to the sand, overcome with thanksgiving.

NINE

The Attack

JUDD and Vicki ran through Jerusalem with the pulsing, flashing cross lighting their way. Judd knew the Unity Army controlled the city, but he didn't care. His Lord was coming, and Judd wanted to see him.

They rounded a corner and noticed several dead bodies. To Judd's amazement, one of them moved. He and Vicki rushed to the man.

When he saw the mark on Judd's and Vicki's foreheads, he smiled. "I was shot and fell here. I pretended I was dead—and nearly was. But just now I felt something strange." He pointed to his chest. "Look. The hole where the bullet went through isn't there."

"We were healed too," Vicki said. She explained where they were going.

"I'll go with you and show you a way

around the Unity Army," the man said. "My name is Ehud."

The three raced into the night, wondering what they would find around the next corner. What would God do to top what he had already done?

Lionel was so excited about his arm that he didn't notice what was happening behind him.

Zeke rushed up and yelled, "You two fall back. They're coming!"

"What?" Lionel said.

But it was too late. The cross in the sky had set something in motion with the Unity Army, and Lionel heard hoofbeats on the sand. He glanced back as horses galloped toward them.

"Big Dog One to all units," someone said over a radio Zeke had on his shoulder. "Hold your fire. Wait. On my command."

"What's he thinking?" Zeke said. Then he hollered at the rebels in front of him, "You heard him—hold your fire!"

The men grumbled, pointing at the oncoming army, a death machine rolling across the desert. The radio crackled with protests.

"Hold, hold, hold!" Big Dog One shouted.

"Permission to speak my mind, sir," someone said.

"Denied. Follow orders."

Lionel backed up while he and Sam watched the human tornado heading straight for them. The front line closed the gap in seconds. In the eerie, yellow light, horsemen pointed rifles. Others wielded swords that glinted yellow off their sharpened edges.

Suddenly, a shot. Then all riders opened fire. Bullets pinged off rocks. Lionel shouted for Zeke to get down, but the man stood tall. The army rushed through the line of rebels, and the lead rider raised his sharpened sword and plunged it down at Zeke.

Lionel put his head in his hands. When he had the courage to look, he saw Zeke still standing. How could the lead rider have missed?

Sam stood, smiling and waving, daring the army to hurt him. He jumped on a rock, both hands in the air, yelling at the top of his lungs.

A rider flicked his sword out and took a swipe at Sam as he passed. If Lionel hadn't seen it, he wouldn't have believed it. It was as if the blade went straight through his friend's body. Sam didn't crumble in pain and blood didn't spurt from his wound, because there was no wound.

Others stood against the gunfire, unhurt by bullets that simply passed through them.

"Come on up!" Sam called to Lionel. "Either these guys are really bad shots, or God's up to something!"

Lionel climbed onto the rock as another wave of riders approached. A man fired at Lionel at close range. When Lionel didn't move, he fired again. The soldier looked at his weapon and paused. Riders swept into him, knocking him from his horse.

Lionel reached down and helped the soldier up.

The man pulled out a pistol and fired again. "Blanks. They're all blanks."

"No," Lionel said, "it's just that your bullets don't work here."

The man turned to run but was caught in the stampede. Horses couldn't take the steep landscape, and those at the front stalled and turned back. Others kept coming, creating a horse traffic jam.

In the chaos, Lionel and Sam climbed down and joined the rebels who calmly walked through the enemy throng.

Zeke found them and slapped Lionel on the back. "We're heading back to the others.

Gonna wait on Jesus with our friends up top rather than down here with the GC."

Sam gave a fake cough and waved a hand in front of his face. "Yeah, these guys are kicking up too much dust."

Conrad and Shelly made it to Enoch's house with others from different hiding places. Charlie had taken Phoenix to Enoch's basement, and the dog was barking his head off.

"You sense it too, don't you, boy?" Conrad said to the shaking dog.

Charlie pulled Phoenix onto his lap and that seemed to help. "You think he knows Jesus is coming?"

"Wouldn't doubt it," Conrad said. "If dogs can sense an earthquake, I'll bet they can sense the King of kings."

"You think he'll get to see Ryan Daley again?" Charlie said. "He's the one who found Phoenix in the first place."

"I hope so."

"What about animals in Jesus' kingdom? Dr. Ben-Judah taught that people could live a long time, even hundreds of years. What does that mean for animals like Phoenix?"

"Well, this is a guess, but I think dogs will live a lot longer, just like people. Dogs and other animals don't have souls, but it does say in the Bible that the wolf and the lamb are going to lie down together."

"And isn't there supposed to be less effects of sin, you know, diseases and sickness and all that?" Charlie said.

"True. Plant life is supposed to grow like crazy, so I wouldn't be surprised if old Phoenix here grew old with the rest of us."

Charlie smiled. "I can't wait to see his reunion with Ryan."

Vicki followed closely behind Judd and Ehud as they made their way through Jerusalem. They rushed down the Via Dolorosa, hit Carpathia Way, and headed for the Damascus Gate. When they found a few Unity Army soldiers there, Ehud led Judd and Vicki east to a breach in the wall and they climbed over.

The cross stayed behind them, lighting the way. Vicki wondered if this was the same kind of light given off by the star announcing Jesus' birth.

They stayed off the main roads, circling the Old City at a safe distance. After they passed a museum, Ehud motioned them northeast to a road renamed Fortunato Boulevard. Vicki chuckled because every block sported a likeness of Leon, the Most High Reverend Father of Carpathianism. Each banner showed him in a different outfit, and in the glowing yellow light, he looked even more ridiculous.

"How much farther?" Judd said.

"Mount Scopus is right this way," Ehud said.

"What if the troops are there?" Vicki said.

"If I'm right, they'll have moved past it, but if not, I know a place where we'll be safe."

Lionel wanted to go to the tech center to see the latest from Chang on Jewish conversions and hear any word from Judd and Vicki, but the stream of people climbing up the side of the mountain changed that. Thousands made their way to the top of a mount overlooking the valley.

"Where's everyone going?" Lionel asked an elderly man who had stopped to catch his breath.

The man pointed up. "The elders . . . they asked us to stay in our groups . . . one hundred groups of a thousand. . . . We'll be going up to the north, over there."

Sam got on one side of the man, Lionel on the other, and they helped him keep up with the others. Lionel was amazed at how orderly everyone was. No one pushed or shoved.

When they reached the top, they helped the man find his place and moved to the edge of the mount. The view of the cross and the Global Community troops was incredible.

"Carpathia's supposed to be out there somewhere," Sam said. "They should be attacking pretty soon."

"Bring it on," Lionel said. "Just means Jesus will come that much sooner."

Conrad and Charlie joined the others gathered in Enoch's backyard. The man usually didn't go outside during the day, but no one seemed afraid. Everyone focused on the sky, wanting to know if they could tell when Jesus returned.

Enoch kept his voice low. "Well, the Bible says the whole world will know when he comes. Revelation 1:7 says, 'Look! He comes with the clouds of heaven. And everyone will see him—even those who pierced him.' "

"How's he gonna 'complish that?" a young man said. "Holy Land's on the other side of the world."

"Don't you think they're seeing what we're seeing now?" Enoch said.

"I guess, but like when the moon is out, people over there see the other side of it, right?"

"They could be seeing the other side of this cross too. We have no idea how massive it is."

"Or if there's more than one," Darrion said.

"How's that?" Enoch said.

"God can do what he wants, right?" she said.

And they all chimed in, some asking questions, others nodding or saying, "Amen."

"He could put ten crosses in the sky to make sure everybody sees one," someone said.

"But there's only one Jesus," another said.

"Yeah, but he can show up anywhere he wants at the same time. Just like he was only one man but he died for everybody, he can appear to everybody too."

"Now you're talking," Enoch said.

"Is he gonna kill a bunch of people here, like he is over there?" Charlie said.

"I'm afraid he is. If they're working for the Antichrist, they're in serious trouble."

Judd noticed signs for a hospital and a university as he followed Ehud and Vicki toward Mount Scopus. He hoped they would make it to the top before the return of Christ.

He wondered about his friends—Jamal,

Lina, and the others he had come to know over the past few months. Had they all been killed? Would he see them again? He pushed the thoughts from his mind and kept going.

"Stop, rebels!" someone yelled behind them.

Judd turned, catching a glimpse of a Unity Army patrol. They rode in an uncovered vehicle, and a soldier aimed a gun at them.

Judd shielded Vicki, and Ehud put up his hands. "You guys run," Judd whispered.

The vehicle drove closer.

"Don't you remember our promise?" Vicki said. "We stick together."

"I'm with you two," Ehud said.

A soldier threw a cigarette on the ground and cursed. "Let's kill them now and get it over with."

"You know our orders," another said.

"Yes, but who's going to know?" the first said. "Just three more heads to chop off later."

A tall man bounded from the vehicle and motioned to the others. "Load them up."

"Where are you taking us?" Judd said as he jumped into the back of the vehicle.

"To the Temple Mount," a soldier said. "You can watch the rest of the rebels die."

As the vehicle pulled out, Judd looked at the pulsing cross in the sky. "Come, Lord Jesus," he whispered.

TEN

The Edge of Time

JUDD thought the Unity soldier might be lying to them about going to the Temple Mount, but that's where they were taken. Along the way, citizens came out of their homes to applaud the soldiers.

They passed several makeshift jails—some inside buildings, others inside barbed-wire fences. It was to one of these outside holding areas that Judd and Vicki were taken. Soldiers took Ehud inside a row of buildings.

"The King is coming!" Ehud shouted as he was led away. "I'll see you when he returns."

Screams came from inside the buildings.

"What is that place?" Vicki said.

Before Judd could answer, a woman behind them spoke. "That's where they torture us, trying to get information about rebels inside the Temple."

The woman, who did not have the mark of the believer, told them about the battles she'd been in and how valiantly the rebels had fought, even against overwhelming odds.

Vicki looked at Judd, and he winked at her. They were thinking the same thing. God had brought them here to reach out to people before the return of Christ.

Lionel stared at the sky and noticed movement on a ledge above. Chaim Rosenzweig and the elders stood where most of the remnant could see them.

"Brothers and sisters in the Messiah," Chaim said. "We gather here in this historic place, this holy city of refuge provided by the Lord God himself. We stand on the precipice of all time with the shadow of history behind us and eternity itself before us, putting all our faith and trust in the rock-solid goodness and strength and majesty of our Savior.

"May the Lord appear as I speak. Oh, the glory of that moment! We stand gazing into the heavens where the promised sign of the Son of Man radiates before us, thundering through the ages the truth that his death on the cross cleanses us from all sin.

"Within the next few minutes, you may see

the enemy of God advancing on this fortified city. I say to you with all the confidence the Father has put in my soul, fear not, for your salvation draweth nigh.

"Now many have asked what is to happen when Antichrist comes against God's chosen people and the Son intervenes. The Bible says he will slay our enemy with a weapon that comes from his mouth. Revelation 1:16 calls it 'a sharp two-edged sword.' Revelation 2:16 quotes him saying that he 'will come to you suddenly and fight against them with the sword of my mouth.' Revelation 19:15 says that 'from his mouth came a sharp sword, and with it he struck down the nations.' And Revelation 19:21 says the army 'was killed by the sharp sword that came out of the mouth of the one riding the white horse.'

"Now let me clarify. I do not believe the Son of God is going to sit on his horse in the clouds with a gigantic sword hanging from his mouth. He is not going to shake his head and slay the millions of Armageddon troops with it. This is clearly a symbolic reference, and if you are a student of the Bible, you know what is meant by a sharp, double-edged sword.

"Hebrews 4:12 says the Word of God 'is full of living power. It is sharper than the sharpest knife, cutting deep into our inner-most thoughts and desires. It exposes us for what we really are.'

"The weapon our Lord and Messiah will use to win the battle and slay the enemy? The Word of God itself! And while the reference to it as a sword may be symbolic, I hold that the description of the result of it is literal. The Word of God is sharp and powerful enough to slay the enemy, literally tearing them asunder."

Lionel felt chills as a million people cheered and applauded. With the cross in the sky, God's remnant around him, and the enemy collected in the valley, Lionel couldn't help but feel the emotion. When someone began singing "A Mighty Fortress Is Our God," he could barely choke out the words.

As the song echoed down the mountain-side, Lionel noticed a motorcade thundering toward them across the desert. Jets screamed overhead, and it looked like Carpathia was ready for the attack.

A Humvee pulled up a steep slope, and someone got out. A light flashed on the man who drew his sword and raised it above his head.

"That's gotta be Carpathia," Sam said.

Singing stopped and everyone looked down on the showy sight. The remnant reacted strongly when Nicolae said, "If there really is a God of Abraham, Isaac, and Jacob, and if he truly has a Son worthy of facing me in combat, I shall destroy him too!"

People gasped.

Nicolae challenged God, daring him to come against his army. It was insane, and yet Carpathia continued. "Be prepared to advance upon Petra on my command. Leave no man, woman, or child alive. The victory is mine, says your living lord and risen king!"

"Let's pray," someone said near Lionel. He bowed his head and prayed. "God, you are the supreme ruler, and you've promised to return and defeat your enemies. I pray you would do that right now."

A murmur of voices rose against the rock walls. Prayers of a million people floated in the air as people joined hands and cried out to God.

Then, with a loud scream, Carpathia ordered his troops to attack. The army surged toward the hill below Lionel and the others. Jet engines roared overhead. Machine guns rattled, cannons fired, grenades and rockets launched, and the remnant in Petra simply stared.

Seconds after the attack came, the pulsing cross in the sky disappeared. Darkness covered the land. A strange clacking sound drifted up from the desert, and Lionel realized the GC's weapons weren't firing. No light came from vehicles or flashlights.

Thousands around Lionel whispered prayers, pleading for Jesus to return.

When the lights went out, Vicki grabbed Judd's arm and stood. They felt their way to the edge of the barbed-wire fence and listened to the anxious voices of the Unity Army officers. The woman Vicki had talked with had prayed with her and asked God's forgiveness for not seeing Jesus as her Messiah. The woman immediately began talking with other prisoners.

"Is this some kind of—?" Judd began, but he stopped.

Light.

Intense white light from heaven covered everything.

It was so bright that GC officers cried out even more than from the darkness.

Vicki glanced up at the thick cloud cover and gasped as it scrolled back. *This is it!* she thought. *This is what we've been waiting for!*

But nothing came from her mouth. She and Judd fell to their knees in awe.

As heaven opened, a white horse appeared. On it sat Jesus, the Messiah, Creator of the universe, Son of God.

Vicki's eyes were riveted on her Savior— right in front of her, his eyes flashing, his head held high. He wore a white robe that stretched to his feet. On the robe were the words: *KING OF KINGS AND LORD OF LORDS.* Around his chest was a golden band. In his right hand were seven stars, and his face shone like the sun. People—a crowd so big it was impossible to count—followed him on white horses.

An angel stepped forward, held out its arms, and beckoned to the birds saying, "Come! Gather together for the great banquet God has prepared. Come and eat the flesh of kings, captains, and strong warriors; of horses and their riders; and of all humanity, both free and slave, small and great."

Then Jesus spoke with a voice that shook the earth. "I am the Alpha and the Omega— the beginning and the end."

Is everyone else seeing this? Vicki wondered. *Is everyone on earth hearing what we're hearing?*

Lionel was thrilled at the voice of Jesus. So this was why Bruce Barnes, Tsion Ben-Judah, and others called it the Glorious Appearing.

Lionel wanted to reach out and thank the Lord for restoring his arm, for hearing his prayers, for saving him from his sins, for his love and justice—for everything!

When Jesus spoke his first words, Lionel glanced at the Unity Army as thousands of soldiers fell like a sea of dominoes. At first, it looked like their bodies sank into the sand, but as Lionel looked closer he noticed bodies ripping open and blood pouring out.

"I am the living one who died. Look, I am alive forever and ever!" Jesus said. "And I hold the keys of death and the grave."

Judd felt like he was in a dream. He had seen people play the part of Jesus, but the real Jesus didn't look or sound like them at all. His voice spoke peace to every part of Judd's heart.

"I am the Son of Man, the Son of God, the Amen—the faithful and true witness, the ruler of God's creation. I am the Lion of the tribe of Judah, the heir to David's throne, the one who conquered to open the scroll and break its seven seals."

Judd glanced at the soldiers around him. They stared, mouths open.

"I am the Lamb that was slain and yet who lives. I am the Shepherd who leads his sheep to the springs of life-giving water. I am the God who will wipe away all your tears. I am your Salvation and Power. I am the Christ who has come for the Accuser, who accused our brothers and sisters before our God day and night, the one who has been thrown down to earth."

Believers looked on in awe and worship while God's enemies whimpered.

Conrad couldn't take his eyes off Jesus. The moment he had waited for since he had asked God to forgive him had finally come. He fell to his knees and soaked in the Lord's presence.

But how was Jesus doing this? How was he appearing to him in Illinois *and* in the Holy Land? And for that matter, Conrad thought, to people around the globe?

"I am the Word of God," Jesus said. "I am Jesus. I am both the source of David and the heir to his throne. I am the bright morning star."

Everyone in Enoch's group remained quiet and listened. Conrad heard soft weeping from Shelly, and he put his arm around her. A commotion next door distracted Conrad for a second when a door opened and neighbors burst from their homes. The light from Christ blinded them, and they ran through the yard, bumping into each other.

"I see him, Mama," little Tolan said, reaching toward the sky.

"That's right," his mother, Lenore, said. "And he sees each one of us down here."

"Where did he get that horse?" Tolan asked.

Lenore smiled and put a finger to her lips, watching Jesus in the sky.

Conrad thought it was a good question. And they had plenty of time to get answers. A thousand years, in fact.

ELEVEN

Death in the Desert

VICKI stared at the heavenly scene, over-whelmed by the sight of Christ. She knew, deep down, that this is what she had been waiting for all her life, not just since she had become a believer. All the drinking and partying, the sneaking out on her parents, all the nights alone—abandoned by her so-called friends—the tears, the sorrow. Jesus was the answer to all her questions, and he was the source of love and everything good. His plan, his life was what she had always needed.

She noticed the people behind Jesus and realized that somewhere back there was her family. Ryan Daley was there too and Pete Davidson and Mark. The list went on and on, and she couldn't wait to see her friends, but that would be later. Right now she focused on the Messiah.

"I am able, once and forever, to save everyone who comes to God through me. I live forever to plead with God on their behalf. I come from above and am above all. My Father has delivered all things to me. God has put all things under my authority, and he gave me this authority for the benefit of the church. I am the anchor of your soul, strong and trustworthy. I am the Lord's Christ."

Vicki had read that Jesus appeared with a sword from his mouth and assumed this sword would be the Word of God. Was Jesus killing his enemies at Petra? What was going on there?

Lionel tore his eyes from Jesus and picked up the high-powered binoculars on the ground. He had to see what was happening on the desert floor.

"I am the vine; you are the branches," Jesus said, his voice booming off the rocks above Lionel. "Those who remain in me, and I in them, will produce much fruit. For apart from me you can do nothing. Anyone who parts from me is thrown away like a useless branch and withers. Such branches are gathered into a pile to be burned.

"I am God's Messenger and High Priest,

appeared in the flesh, righteous by the Spirit, seen by angels, announced to the nations, believed on in the world, taken up into heaven.

"I am the Son whom God has promised everything to as an inheritance, and through whom he made the universe and everything in it. I reflect God's own glory, and everything about me represents God exactly. I sustain the universe by the mighty power of my command. After I died to cleanse you from the stain of sin, I sat down in the place of honor at the right hand of the majestic God of heaven. I am far greater than the angels, just as the name God gave me is far greater than their names."

Lionel scanned the battlefield and was amazed at the amount of blood. Some soldiers saw their fallen comrades and were so upset they turned their guns on themselves. Others dug into the blood-soaked sand, trying to find a place to hide from the white light of God.

The army—at least those still alive—ran away from Jesus. But where were they going? Where could anyone go from the gaze of almighty God?

Lionel remembered comforting words from the Psalms: "I can never escape from your Spirit! I can never get away from your presence!" Now that verse took on new meaning. Where could any enemy go to get away from God's judgment?

As the rest of the living fled, Lionel scanned the perimeter of Petra. For miles he saw dead and dying soldiers, holes in the sand where trucks and tanks lay buried, dead horses, and a few skeleton-like people walking in a daze. Above this awful scene circled a huge flock of birds. They flew to the bodies and began eating.

In the lull that followed, someone began singing, "Praise God from whom all blessings flow. . . ." It was Mr. Stein, standing with Chaim and the elders. Soon a million others joined their song of praise.

Conrad had imagined this moment a thousand times. He had pictured Jesus riding on a horse the size of an airplane, running about ten feet off the ground, his hair trailing in the wind. He'd also dreamed of a hundred-foot-tall Jesus walking toward Jerusalem, smashing things like monsters did in horror movies. But Conrad had never imagined anything like this. It was as if Jesus had come for Conrad alone and was looking straight at him.

"Just fellowship with your Savior," Enoch said quietly.

Jesus said, "Keep your eyes on me, on whom your faith depends from start to finish. I was willing to die a shameful death on the cross because of the joy I knew would be mine afterward. Now I am seated in the place of highest honor beside God's throne in heaven.

"Now God commands everyone everywhere to turn away from idols and turn to him. For he has set a day for judging the world with justice by the man he has appointed, and he proved to everyone who this is by raising me from the dead.

"I am Jesus Christ, the one who pleases God completely. I am the sacrifice for your sins. I take away not only your sins but the sins of all the world. God raised me to life. And you are witnesses of this fact! I am the Word that became human and lived here on earth among you. I am full of unfailing love and faithfulness. And you have seen my glory, the glory of the only Son of the Father.

"Though I am God, I did not demand and cling to my rights as God. I made myself nothing; I took the humble position of a slave and appeared in human form. And in human form I obediently humbled myself even further by dying a criminal's death on a cross.

"Because of this, Conrad, God raised me up to the heights of heaven and gave me a name that is above every other name, so that at the name of Jesus every knee will bow, in heaven and on earth and under the earth, and every tongue will confess that Jesus Christ is Lord, to the glory of God the Father."

People around Conrad wept.

"Did you hear that?" Enoch said. "He used my name."

"He used *my* name too," Conrad said, still unable to believe it.

"He called me by name," Josey Fogarty said.

Charlie rushed to Conrad and Shelly. "He talked to me too!"

Vicki glanced at Judd, and by the look on his face she could tell he had heard his name too. When Jesus had used her name, she almost blushed, almost felt guilty. Then she realized this was going on with each believer.

"Vicki," Jesus said, "you know my love and kindness, that though I was very rich, yet for your sake I became poor, so that by my poverty I could make you rich.

"I have rescued you from the one who rules in the kingdom of darkness, and I have brought you into the Kingdom of God's dear Son. I have purchased your freedom with my blood and have forgiven all your sins.

"I am the one through whom God created everything in heaven and earth. I made the things you can see and the things you can't see—kings, kingdoms, rulers, and authorities. Everything has been created through me and for me. I existed before everything else began, and I hold all creation together.

"I am the head of the church, which is my body. I am the first of all who will rise from the dead, so I am first in everything. For God in all his fullness was pleased to live in me, and by me God reconciled everything to himself. I made peace with everything in heaven and on earth by means of my blood on the cross."

Vicki leaned against a post holding the barbed wire and whispered, "Jesus, I don't deserve the things you've done for me."

"And you, Vicki, were once so far away from God. You were his enemy, separated from him by your evil thoughts and actions, yet now I have brought you back as his friend. I have done this through my death on the cross in my own human body. As a result, I have brought you into the very presence of God, and you are holy and blameless as you stand before him without a single fault."

After Jesus stopped speaking, Lionel walked with Sam and found Mr. Stein. They both had many questions, and Mr. Stein tried to answer them.

"Didn't Dr. Rosenzweig say the remnant was supposed to go to Jerusalem, back to their home city?" Sam said.

"He did," Mr. Stein said.

"But how?" Lionel said. "There's no way to transport a million people."

"Ah, have you forgotten whose battle this is?" Mr. Stein said, pointing at Jesus. "If God wants us in Israel, he will make a way. Now the elders have asked us to head down the mountain—"

Mr. Stein stopped when Jesus spoke again in a loud voice. "Someday, O Israel, I will gather the few of you who are left. I will bring you together again like sheep in a fold, like a flock in its pasture. Yes, your land will again be filled with noisy crowds!

"I, your leader, will break out and lead you out of exile. I will bring you through the gates of your cities of captivity, back to your own land. I, your king, will lead you; I, the Lord, will guide you."

People rushed down the mountainside. Mr. Stein kept up with Lionel and Sam, scurrying along the rocks and pathways made over the past few months.

Lionel paused, looking up at Petra, wondering if they were leaving it forever. In the distance dust clouds rose from the crowds. Were the people driving ATVs? Had God provided a way to Jerusalem? He turned to Mr. Stein.

"We're not going to Jerusalem yet," Mr. Stein said. "The Lord is taking us to the next battle—there will be three more, according to Dr. Rosenzweig."

As they reached the desert floor, people around them laughed and talked about following Jesus. Were they going to walk? Many of the remnant were small children, and others were elderly.

Lionel stared at the dust and shook his head. He had just seen thousands of the enemy killed by Jesus' words, and he was concerned about a sixty-mile trip?

Sam had wandered ahead and now ran back. "Come on. Run with us."

"What do you mean?" Lionel said, but Sam pulled at his arm, making Lionel go faster. Lionel glanced up at Jesus who looked back and smiled, seeming to urge him on.

Lionel broke into a jog, and soon he was sprinting along with Sam, jumping over GC bodies and weapons, his feet barely touching the ground. He was moving faster than a human was supposed to run.

Lionel had done a research project in middle school about how fast humans could run. He had come up with a maximum speed of 27 miles per hour for sprinters, and an average speed of between 15 to 20 mph for those running distances of any kind.

But there was no way he was going 15 miles per hour now. Or even 30. Objects on the ground were a blur! And it wasn't only healthy young people going fast—it was all ages. Youngsters just out of diapers ran next to Lionel. And Mr. Stein was not far away, grinning and laughing. God was providing the speed. All Lionel had to do was work his legs.

"It's like riding a bike for two!" Mr. Stein called. "The Lord is the one doing the pedaling. We just have to get on and follow!"

The sensation of running three and maybe four times as fast as a human had ever run made Lionel laugh out loud. His feet moved faster, but his strides, instead of being a yard, took in ten feet with each step. The amazing thing was, Lionel didn't feel out of breath. His strength kept coming like the manna that fell every day.

Thirty minutes later, Lionel and his friends neared the town of Bozrah. The rest of the million inside Petra had arrived as well, drawn to the scene by Jesus himself.

Unity Army troops stood before them, looking haggard and tired. Huge sweat stains fouled their uniforms while the people from Petra looked like they had just returned from lunch at an air-conditioned restaurant.

"What happens now?" Lionel said.

Mr. Stein motioned to the depleted army. "I think they're foolish enough to attack."

TWELVE

Surprise for Lionel

LIONEL couldn't believe it when the Unity Army moved forward and unleashed everything they had on the unarmed men, women, and children. Soldiers at the front aimed guns and fired, while troops behind launched missiles, rockets, and mortars. The noise was deafening and the flash of fire was blinding, but every time a missile or rocket hit, even in the midst of the people, no one was hurt.

Lionel looked to his Savior. Over the roar of the battle, Jesus' voice could be heard clearly. "Come hear and listen, O nations of the earth. Let the world and everything in it hear my words. For the Lord is enraged against the nations. His fury is against all their armies. He will completely destroy them, bringing about their slaughter."

As soon as Jesus spoke, soldiers and horses exploded. Lionel grabbed a pair of binoculars and looked closer. He focused on a soldier firing his weapon toward the remnant. The man's eyes grew wide, and he lowered his gun. Then his face bloated and turned red, as if his blood were boiling. The next second, the man's body blew into a million pieces, as did those around him.

"Their dead will be left unburied, and the stench of rotting bodies will fill the land. The mountains will flow with their blood. The heavens above will melt away and disappear like a rolled-up scroll. The stars will fall from the sky, just as withered leaves and fruit fall from a tree."

Lionel again focused on the nearest soldiers. They threw down their weapons and dropped to their knees. Some shoved fists in the air at Christ, cursing him before they died. Instead of exploding, these were sliced in two, and their insides poured onto the desert floor. When those behind them saw, they turned to run, but the same thing happened to them. They were cut in two where they stood, and their blood gushed.

"When my sword has finished its work in the heavens, then watch," Jesus said. "It will fall upon Edom, the nation I have completely destroyed. The sword of the Lord is drenched with blood. It is covered with fat as though it had been used for killing lambs and goats and rams for sacrifice. Yes, the Lord will offer a great sacrifice in the rich city of Bozrah. He will make a mighty slaughter in Edom. The land will be soaked with blood and the soil enriched with fat."

Now the army fell like red sticks. Lionel couldn't tell whether Christ's judgment was coming from the air or from the earth as men and women who had pledged their lives to Carpathia were cut down.

An aircraft of some sort screamed in and landed at the other side of the slaughtered army. It was a jet helicopter, and someone mentioned it was for Nicolae.

The firing stopped. Except for the chopper, everything was deathly still. The craft lifted off and headed north, leaving the remnant to stare out on the valley of blood.

Sam touched Lionel's shoulder. "Look! The Lord Jesus is coming down."

The King of kings landed and dismounted from his white horse. He walked through the battlefield, the hem of his robe turning red from the blood of the enemy.

The army of heaven that hovered above him began to speak in unison. "Who is this who comes from Edom, from the city of

Bozrah, with his clothing stained red? Who is this in royal robes, marching in the greatness of his strength?"

Jesus answered, "It is I, the Lord, announcing your salvation! It is I, the Lord, who is mighty to save!"

"Why are your clothes so red, as if you have been treading out grapes?" they asked.

"I have trodden the winepress alone; no one was there to help me," Jesus said. "In my anger I have trampled my enemies as if they were grapes. In my fury I have trampled my foes. It is their blood that has stained my clothes. For the time has come for me to avenge my people, to ransom them from their oppressors.

"I looked, but no one came to help my people. I was amazed and appalled at what I saw. So I executed vengeance alone; unaided, I passed down judgment. I crushed the nations in my anger and made them stagger and fall to the ground."

The conversation continued back and forth until Jesus turned toward the remnant in Bozrah. "When you see Jerusalem surrounded by armies, then you will know that the time of its destruction has arrived. Then those in Judea must flee to the hills. Let those in Jerusalem escape, and those outside the city should not enter it for shelter.

"For those will be the days of God's vengeance, and the prophetic words of the Scriptures will be fulfilled. . . . So when all these things begin to happen, stand straight and look up, for your salvation is near!"

Judd watched Jesus sink from view, then looked at Vicki. The light of Jesus was still there and, he assumed, could be seen all over the world. But they couldn't see the Lord anymore.

"What do you think's happening?" Judd said.

"Not sure," Vicki said. "But there's no doubt he'll be heading this way soon. If Tsion was right, Jesus will overcome the enemy as he reaches Mount Megiddo. Then he's coming here."

"But Jerusalem's going to fall, right?" Judd said.

Vicki nodded. "I'm just not sure what that means. The GC will take the Temple Mount, but whether they kill everybody or not . . ."

Judd glanced at the guards standing nearby. These soldiers had been as fascinated with the return of Jesus as anyone.

"What's that guy over there doing?" Vicki whispered.

A soldier had run in from the direction of the Temple Mount and now spoke with a higher ranking official. They gestured toward the prisoners, and Judd strained to hear their conversation.

". . . and we've now surrounded the entire city," the soldier said. "Our forces are massed from west of the Dead Sea to the Valley of Megiddo."

"We're in good shape then," the officer said.

"Except for the casualties in Edom—"

"Stop!" The officer drew close and warned the soldier not to talk about any loss of life on the Unity Army side.

"Sorry, sir," the soldier said. "But you need to know about the unrest."

"What are you talking about?"

"Our troops are hungry. There are rumors that there are no reinforcements—"

"They're wrong!" the officer shouted, his face turning red with rage. "And don't count our southern troops out yet."

"—and you know how long it's been since we've been paid."

"A Unity Army soldier doesn't perform this work for the pay. We serve in the interests of peace, and that is our payment. We ultimately serve the risen Lord Carpathia."

"Yes, of course, sir. Still, you can understand why they're upset. And now, with having to take prisoners . . ."

The two men looked at the holding area.

"I don't like the way they're looking at us," Vicki said.

Judd put an arm around her. "It's okay. Jesus will be here soon." But inside, Judd agreed with her. He didn't like the looks of this either.

For the next few hours, Lionel and a million others followed Jesus, who was again riding his horse. The people ran through the desert at lightning speed, watching Jesus ahead of them and the heavenly army above.

Lionel's heart leaped when Jesus spoke, his voice sounding as if he were standing right next to him. "I am the King who comes in the name of the Lord. I mediate the new covenant between God and people. I personally carried away your sins in my own body on the cross so you can be dead to sin and live for what is right.

"I am the true bread of God who came down from heaven and gives life to the world. So let us celebrate the festival, not by eating the old bread of wickedness and evil, but by eating the new bread of my purity and truth."

Lionel had read the Bible for many years and recognized the things Jesus was saying as words taken directly from Scripture. Still, hearing Jesus speak thrilled him. Just when Lionel thought things couldn't get any better, Jesus spoke directly to him.

"Lionel, I came to bring truth to the world. All who love the truth recognize that what I say is true. I assure you, I can do nothing by myself. I do only what I see the Father doing. Whatever the Father does, I also do. I am the stone that the builders rejected and have now become the cornerstone."

All Lionel could do was say, "Thank you" each time Jesus spoke to him. He couldn't think of anything else, and it seemed to make Jesus smile.

"Where are we going?" Lionel said to Sam.

"Wherever Jesus leads," Sam said. "I don't pretend to know what's going to happen, but if we follow the Lord, we will be in just the right place at the right time."

Lionel couldn't get over the sight of old men and women running so fast. In Petra these people had walked slowly, hunched over, some using canes, others walking from rock to rock, careful of their footing. Now they were upright, running faster than Olympic athletes.

They continued north, following Jesus,

listening to his words. A portion of Carpathia's army fell dead as Jesus passed them.

"Lionel, take my yoke upon you," Jesus said. "Let me teach you, because I am humble and gentle, and you will find rest for your soul. For my yoke fits perfectly, and the burden I give you is light."

As the group moved farther, the Unity Army seemed to be dug in and waiting. The GC no doubt believed they would have a great victory.

The remnant bypassed Israel, far to their left, and headed toward Megiddo, or the Valley of Armageddon. At one point, Jesus said, "I give you eternal life, Lionel, and you will never perish. No one will snatch you away from me, for my Father has given you to me, and he is more powerful than anyone else. So no one can take you from me. The Father and I are one.

"I am leaving you with a gift—peace of mind and heart. And the peace I give isn't like the peace the world gives. So don't be troubled or afraid."

Lionel recalled the verse that said, "If God is for us, who can ever be against us?" He had never felt the truth of it so clearly.

Jesus seemed to go ahead of them faster, leaving the remnant behind. Lionel and the others slowed, then stopped north of Jerusalem. No one seemed tired, but it was clear that Jesus wanted them to stay.

"Looks like we won't need to do any more work for Zeke," Sam said.

"I have to tell you," Lionel said, "I didn't like our jobs very much."

"What do you think you'll be doing once the kingdom begins?"

Lionel shrugged. "Whatever needs to be done, I guess. I'm not picky."

Sam looked away. Lionel asked if something was wrong, and Sam nodded. "I was just thinking about my father. You're going to see your family again. I'll see my mom, but not my dad."

Lionel put an arm around him. "I understand. I had an uncle who I tried to talk to after the Rapture. He knew the truth, but he died before he could pray."

"How do you know for sure?" Sam said. "Were you with him?"

"No, Judd and I found him—"

"Then he could have asked God's forgiveness."

"You don't know my uncle André," Lionel said.

Lionel fell silent as Jesus spoke again. "No one has ever seen God. I, his only Son, who am myself God, am near to the Father's heart;

I have told you about him. I am called the Son of the Most High. And the Lord God will give me the throne of my ancestor David."

Another voice came from heaven. "Look at my Servant, whom I have chosen. He is my Beloved, and I am very pleased with him. I will put my Spirit upon him, and he will proclaim justice to the nations."

Sam's eyes grew wide. "You think that was God the Father?"

"I can't imagine who else," Lionel said.

Jesus answered: "The law was given through Moses; God's unfailing love and faithfulness come through me. Now, Lionel, may the God of peace, who brought me from the dead, equip you with all you need for doing his will. May he produce in you all that is pleasing to him. Amen."

On the last word, the people fell to their knees, praising God. Lionel kept his head down, thanking God and worshiping him.

Then the noise of battle wafted over the desert. Jesus spoke, and even from this distance Lionel heard soldiers wailing.

A few minutes later, another great flock of birds appeared in the sky. Lionel guessed this was not good news for Nicolae and his army.

THIRTEEN

Carpathia's Parade

THE temperature dropped quickly around Lionel and the others, then returned to normal. News reached them of a great hailstorm—with chunks of ice weighing a hundred pounds or more—that had fallen on the massacred Unity Army. Water mingled with blood, creating a red, gooey liquid that was four feet deep in some places.

Fresh from battle, Jesus addressed the remnant. "You belong to God, my dear children. You have already won your fight with these false prophets, because the Spirit who lives in you is greater than the spirit who lives in the world. These people belong to this world, so they speak from the world's viewpoint, and the world listens to them. But you belong to God; that is why those who know God listen to you. That is how you know if someone has the Spirit of truth or the spirit of deception.

"Dear friends, continue to love one another, for love comes from God. Anyone who loves is born of God and knows God. But anyone who does not love does not know God—for God is love. God showed how much he loved you by sending his only Son into the world so that you might have eternal life through him. This is real love. It is not that you loved God, but that he loved you and sent me as a sacrifice to take away your sins.

"Lionel, since God loved you that much, you surely ought to love each other."

As Jesus spoke, people slowly turned toward Jerusalem. Jesus moved ahead of them, his horse galloping onward until Lionel lost sight of him.

Judd watched the soldiers huddle together to stay warm through the icy blast. When things warmed, a number of citizens strolled through the thousands of soldiers. Rebels still held the Temple Mount as far as Judd could tell, but the Unity Army seemed content to let them have it for now. A radio crackled with news that the potentate was on his way, and soldiers snapped to attention.

Soon loudspeakers boomed Nicolae's voice through the area. "As we approach what many have referred to as the Eternal City, I am pleased to announce that following our victory here, this shall become the new Global Community headquarters. My palace shall be rebuilt on the site of the ruins of the temple, the destruction of which is on our agenda."

Carpathia continued, predicting a total takeover of Jerusalem. Judd couldn't believe it when the man referred to Jesus as "this one who flits about in the air quoting ancient fairy-tale texts." Nicolae predicted Jesus would die. "He is no match for the risen lord of this world and for the fighting force in place to face him. It does not even trouble me to make public our plan, as it has already succeeded. This city and these despicable people have long been his chosen ones, so we have forced him to show himself, to declare himself, to vainly try to defend them or be shown for the fraud and coward that he is. Either he attempts to come to their rescue or they will see him for who he really is and reject him as an impostor. Or he will foolishly come against my immovable force and me and prove once and for all who is the better man."

Though Judd expected this speech of

Nicolae's to encourage the troops, the soldiers nearby seemed unaffected. No yelling, screaming, or shouting Nicolae's support.

"My pledge to you, loyal citizens of the Global Community," Carpathia said, "is that come the end of this battle, no opponent of my leadership and regime will remain standing, yea, not one will be left alive. The only living beings on planet Earth will be trustworthy citizens, lovers of peace and harmony and tranquility, which I offer with love for all from the depths of my being.

"I am but ten miles west of Jerusalem as we speak, and I will be dismissing my cabinet and generals so they may be about the business of waging this conflict under my command. The Most High Reverend of Carpathianism, Dr. Leon Fortunato himself, will serve as my chauffeur for my triumphal entry. Citizens are already lining the roadway to greet me, and I thank you for your support."

A few minutes later, drums and trumpets sounded in the distance. Vicki, who had buried her head in Judd's chest, looked up. "Carpathia has mocked everything God's done. This is his version of the triumphal entry."

"Let him enjoy it," Judd muttered. "He doesn't have much longer."

A young officer spoke to his superior. "Sir,

we could present these prisoners to the potentate for execution. Those without the mark could be beheaded in front of him as a sacrifice."

The commanding officer glanced at the prisoners, then waved a hand. "That can come after the victory."

"They're going after the rebels at the Temple Mount," Vicki said. "Sounds like Carpathia's gonna lead the charge."

"Let him come," Judd said, sneaking a peek at the sky. Jesus and his heavenly army were nowhere in sight.

Lionel and Sam joined the others on a hill overlooking Jerusalem. The sky cleared as Carpathia paraded through Jerusalem.

Someone pulled out a handheld TV and caught GCNN's coverage of Nicolae riding a stallion, his sword raised in the air. He swung it, and the troops around him whooped. "Follow me to the Western Wall and make way for the battering ram and missile launchers! Upon my command, open fire!"

Lionel couldn't help thinking of Judd and Vicki. Though he knew they would see each other again soon, he hated the thought of them being killed in Jerusalem. "Lord Jesus, protect my friends until we see each other again."

Since Jesus had appeared, Lionel's attitude toward prayer had taken on a new dimension. Instead of just saying, "Amen," Lionel looked up and listened for an answer.

Vicki heard the oncoming army and shuddered. The others in the holding area moved toward the barbed wire.

"Don't get any ideas," a soldier said, waving an Uzi at them. "I'll mow all of you down."

Some civilians stood on a wall behind them pointing and cheering as hundreds of horses clip-clopped their way toward the Temple Mount.

"Here he comes!" a woman shouted, then broke into a not-so-stirring rendition of "Hail Carpathia."

The woman stopped when Nicolae shouted orders. Mounted soldiers urged their horses forward but they reared and bucked, spinning into each other. Some ran headlong into the wall. One horse and rider headed straight for the barbed-wire enclosure. The armed guard fell under the horse's hooves while the animal flung itself into the makeshift prison.

Quickly, the prisoners climbed over the

downed wire, only to be met by three Unity Army soldiers holding guns. Vicki and Judd took a step back, still inside the prison.

"No!" Vicki screamed as the soldiers aimed their guns.

But before they could shoot, skin dripped from their arms and their eyes melted. The once-healthy soldiers were now simply uniforms full of bones. Seconds later the same thing happened to the horses. Their flesh and eyes and tongues dripped away like candle wax.

Vicki was too stunned to move. She had read verses in Revelation that said this was going to happen. She had even seen people die from the horsemen of terror and stung by the demon locusts, but she had never seen anything so gruesome. Without a shot fired or a missile launched, the Unity Army melted into the street.

"Look over there," Judd said.

Leon had his face in his hands and knelt. Nicolae Carpathia, God's archenemy, ordered Leon Fortunato to his feet. "Get up, Leon! Get up! We are not defeated! We have a million more soldiers and we shall prevail!"

Leon just whimpered and wailed.

Carpathia cursed God and lifted his sword

to the sky. Then he paused, seeing something in the heavens.

Vicki glanced up when God's temple opened and a flood of brilliant light surrounded her.

Judd pulled Vicki toward a nearby wall as lightning flashed, thunder roared, and the earth shifted.

In seconds the earth buckled and swayed. Carpathia's soldiers were swallowed through great cracks in the earth.

Conrad held on to Shelly while they rode out the huge earthquake together. Somehow the Global Community News Network managed to stay on the air and showed satellite pictures of the earth bathed in a light that originated from Jesus. In North America, a huge dust cloud hovered over Arizona, and reports that the Grand Canyon had been filled in and was now level brought *oohs* and *aahs* from their friends. Even more incredible was the shot over Nepal showing that Mount Everest and the mountain ranges surrounding it had crumbled and were now as flat as every other place on earth. Islands disappeared into the sea. Everything had been leveled except for the city of Jerusalem.

Someone gasped and pointed up. Conrad glanced skyward and saw Jesus, who spoke in a loud voice. "Speak tenderly to Jerusalem. Tell her that her sad days are gone and that her sins are pardoned. Yes, the Lord has punished her in full for all her sins.

"Fill the valleys and level the hills. Straighten out the curves and smooth off the rough spots. Then the glory of the Lord will be revealed, and all people will see it together. The Lord has spoken!

"Watch, for the day of the Lord has come when your possessions will be plundered right in front of you! On that day I gathered all the nations to fight against Jerusalem. Half the population was taken away into captivity, and half was left among the ruins of the city. I went out and fought against those nations, as I have fought in times past.

"And I sent a plague on all the nations that fought against Jerusalem. Their people became like walking corpses, their flesh rotting away. Their eyes shriveled in their sockets, and their tongues decayed in their mouths. On that day they were terrified, stricken by me with great panic.

"I made Jerusalem and Judah like an intoxicating drink to all the nearby nations that sent their armies to besiege Jerusalem. On that day I made Jerusalem a heavy stone, a burden for the world. None of the nations who tried to lift it escaped unscathed.

"I caused every horse to panic and every rider to lose his nerve. I watched over the people of Judah, but I blinded the horses of her enemies.

"I defended the people of Jerusalem; the weakest among them will be as mighty as King David! And the royal descendants will be like God, like the angel of the Lord who goes before them! I destroyed all the nations that came against Jerusalem.

"Therefore, a curse consumed the earth and its people. They were left desolate, destroyed by fire. Few were left alive.

"Throughout the earth the story is the same—like the stray olives left on the tree or the few grapes left on the vine after harvest, only a remnant is left.

"That group called on my name, and I answered them. I said, 'These are my people,' and they said, 'The Lord is our God.' "

Lionel followed the others to the east side of the Old City. Only a small portion of Carpathia's army remained alive, and most of them had been injured. Piles of human bones stood several feet high in some places. Many of the living staggered toward shelter as Jesus sat on his white horse. A host of his army was behind him looking on at the one-sided victory.

"It's going to be hard to get used to everything being flat," Sam said.

Lionel smiled and looked at the sky. "There's going to be a lot of things around here that *won't* be hard to get used to."

FOURTEEN

Personal Words

JUDD was proud of Vicki for having the idea of finding their new friend Ehud and releasing him. They crept through the narrow street, avoiding the surviving Unity Army soldiers, and found several dozen Jewish believers chained together in a basement of a two-story building. Ehud called to them and said many of the prisoners had been starved and tortured, but they all looked fine now. Judd noticed bones of a guard near a vending machine and fished through the man's pockets until he heard keys rattle.

While Vicki loosed the prisoners, Judd smashed the vending machine and handed out food. Vicki wanted to look for more prisoners, but Judd thought it wouldn't be safe with the Unity Army still around.

"How long before we see the Messiah

return to the Mount of Olives?" a skinny prisoner said to the others.

When no one answered Vicki said, "It has to be soon. It looks like he's already taken care of most of Carpathia's troops."

Ehud ran away with the other prisoners while Judd and Vicki moved through a gate and toward a hillside. Judd thought she looked as happy as he had seen her in months.

"Why is the Mount of Olives so important?" Judd said.

Vicki started to answer. Then her jaw dropped. "Look, the remnant is moving this way."

Lionel left Sam and the rest of the remnant and jogged toward Jerusalem. When he reached the wall of the city, he climbed on top and scanned the area. Bodies lay strewn about the streets. Dead rebels were scattered among the bones of Unity Army soldiers. Surviving soldiers regrouped for another attack on the Temple Mount.

He wondered where the bodies of Dr. Ben-Judah and Buck Williams were. Perhaps Buck and Tsion were mixed in with the other dead in front of him.

Lionel scampered down from the wall and

raced back to his friends. He was thrilled that he would be face-to-face with Jesus again soon.

Conrad and Shelly helped Enoch move his furniture from the basement to the first floor of his house. Enoch said there would be no more hiding now that the Lord had returned. Shelly called for them from upstairs, where they found Nicolae Carpathia and Leon Fortunato on television, surrounded by advisors, generals, and a swarm of reporters.

"You'd think he'd have enough sense to get out of there," Enoch said.

"Denial's not just a dried-up river in Egypt," Conrad said.

"That was bad," Shelly said, punching Conrad on the shoulder.

Carpathia waved his arms and barked orders at troops. Conrad turned up the volume in time to hear Nicolae say, "This city shall become my throne. The temple will be flattened and the way made for my palace, the most magnificent structure ever erected. We have captured half the enemy here, and we will dispose of the other half in due time.

"The final stage of our conquest is nearly

ready to be executed, and we will soon be rid of this nuisance from above."

Lionel looked up and saw Jesus hovering over the remnant. He spoke words of comfort and compassion, and when Lionel fell to his knees, Jesus spoke directly to him. "It has pleased God to tell his people that the riches and glory of Christ are for you, Lionel. Christ lives in you, and this is your assurance that you will share in his glory. I am a mighty Savior from the royal line of God's servant David. The truth is, I existed before Abraham was even born!"

The remnant burst into praises to Jesus, drowning out the sound of the marching band that played "Hail Carpathia" in the distance.

Lionel moved along the edges of the crowd, watching Jesus.

Behind him a familiar voice said, "He's blinded to the truth about himself and God. He's leading every one of those soldiers to certain death."

Lionel turned and saw Judd and Vicki. He put his left arm behind his back and yelled for them.

Their faces lit up when they saw Lionel, and they rushed toward him.

"Wait. I have a surprise," Lionel said, pulling his left arm from behind his back. Vicki and Judd were amazed at what God had done, and they hugged Lionel.

"Can you believe we're actually here?" Vicki said. "I've dreamed of this moment since we met in Bruce Barnes' office at New Hope Village Church."

"And we're together." Lionel began to tell them about his experience running from Petra to Jerusalem, but when Jesus nudged his horse forward to the Mount of Olives, he stopped. The remnant stood and Carpathia headed toward them, his sword held high, the rest of his army trailing.

Jesus dismounted as Carpathia shouted the command to attack. As soldiers fired and horses galloped forward, Jesus' voice sounded like a trumpet. "I AM THE ONE WHO ALWAYS IS."

Immediately the Mount of Olives split in two. The newly formed chasm left Carpathia and his army on one side, Jesus and the remnant on the other. The firing and galloping stopped. Soldiers screamed in agony, and their bodies burst open.

Jesus spoke to those still held prisoner in Jerusalem. "You will flee through this valley, for it will reach across to Azal. Yes, you will flee as you did from the earthquake in the days of King Uzziah of Judah. Then the Lord your God will come, and all his holy ones with me."

People inside Jerusalem shouted, and Vicki put a hand to her mouth. "Look," she whispered.

Out of the gates came prisoners, some with chains still on their feet. Their bodies were thin and many had scars, but they ran toward the valley created when the mount had split. The earth rumbled, and Lionel stared as the whole city of Jerusalem rose higher and higher into the air until it stood thirty yards above everything.

Judd tapped Lionel's shoulder and pointed toward two figures running for their lives. "That's Nicolae and Leon, but what's that bright thing bouncing ahead of them?"

Lionel shrugged. "They say that Satan disguises himself as an angel of light. Maybe that's old Lucifer."

Unity Army soldiers chased the freed captives through the new valley. But when Jesus spoke, the soldiers fell dead.

"Life-giving waters will flow out from Jerusalem," Jesus said, "half toward the Dead Sea and half toward the Mediterranean, flowing continuously both in summer and in winter. And the Lord will be king over all the earth.

Today there will be one Lord—his name alone will be worshiped.

"All the land from Geba, north of Judah, to Rimmon, south of Jerusalem, has become one vast plain. But Jerusalem has been raised up in its original place and inhabited all the way from the Benjamin Gate over to the site of the old gate, then to the Corner Gate, and from the Tower of Hananel to the king's wine-presses. And Jerusalem will be filled, safe at last, never again to be cursed and destroyed."

Tears came to Vicki's eyes when Jesus mounted his horse and rode on. Every word he spoke devoured his enemies.

"This is the day of God's vengeance, and the prophetic words of the Scriptures have been fulfilled. The arrogance of all people will be brought low. Their pride will lie in the dust. The Lord alone will be exalted!"

Voices from heaven shouted, "The whole world has now become the Kingdom of our Lord and of his Christ, and he will reign forever and ever.

"We give thanks to you, Lord God Almighty, the one who is and who always was, for now you have assumed your great power and have begun to reign. The nations were angry with you, but now the time of your wrath has come. It is time to judge the dead and reward your servants. You will reward your prophets and your holy people, all who fear your name, from the least to the greatest. And you will destroy all who have caused destruction on the earth."

As Vicki followed the people, she expected to see dead bodies about the streets and fallen weapons and equipment. Instead, as the remnant sang and danced and praised God, she saw clean streets and no bodies. And something else strange—all the walls had been leveled.

"There is only one God and one Mediator who can reconcile God and people, I, the man Christ Jesus. I gave my life to purchase freedom for everyone."

People lined up for miles behind Jesus, and finally they all were inside the city. Hovering over them were the hosts of heaven, still on horseback. Judd grabbed Vicki's arm, she grabbed Lionel, and they moved to a ledge overlooking the crowd.

Jesus had dismounted and stretched out his arms. "O Jerusalem, Jerusalem," the Lord cried, "the city that kills the prophets and stones God's messengers! How often I have wanted to gather your children together as a hen protects her chicks beneath her wings, but you wouldn't let me. And now look, your house is left to you empty. And you will never see me again until you say, 'Bless the one who comes in the name of the Lord!' "

Vicki had held her breath for so long, but now she couldn't help bursting forth, "Bless the one who comes in the name of the Lord!"

Everyone else had shouted the same thing at the same time, and Jesus beamed.

Judd looked around at people from different backgrounds who spoke different languages. He put his head in his hands and whispered, "Thank you, Jesus. Thank you for letting us be here at this moment."

When he looked up, five heavenly beings stood behind Jesus. Vicki nudged Judd and said, "The second one from the left is the one we saw in Wisconsin."

People around them spoke the angels' names. Nahum, Christopher, and Caleb had been angels of mercy, delivering some from certain death. The two other angels near Jesus were Gabriel and Michael.

Judd looked into Jesus' eyes, and something stirred in his heart. Jesus said, "Come to me, my child."

Judd's mouth dropped open, and he put a hand to his chest. "Me?"

Jesus nodded.

Judd looked at Vicki. She and Lionel moved forward with him. The whole throng moved toward Jesus as he spoke to a million people individually. Incredible!

"Come to me, Judd, and I will give you rest."

Judd kept moving, wanting to run into the arms of Jesus like a child, but he couldn't stop thinking about his sin. He had been so selfish and felt dirty, as if Jesus might reject him.

But the Lord reached out with his scarred hands. "Come," he said softly.

Judd looked into Jesus' eyes—burning like fire and so loving. He ran into the arms of Christ and was gathered in.

"Judd, Judd, how I have looked forward to and longed for this day. I knew your name before the foundation of the world. I have prepared a place for you, and if it were not so, I would have told you."

Judd tried to speak but couldn't.

Jesus gently pushed Judd back and looked him full in the face. Judd was only inches away from the King of kings. "I was there when you were born. I was there the night at the youth group when you decided you would go your own way."

"Forgive me . . . ," Judd choked.

Vicki stared into the eyes of love and wept.

"Vicki, I was there when you cried yourself

to sleep. When your uncle caused you so much pain. I was there when your mother and father chose me and you rejected me."

"I'm so sorry. . . ."

"I was there when you were left behind. I was there when you first met Judd. And I was waiting when you heard the truth and finally came to me."

Vicki cocked her head, and a tear ran down her cheek. "Oh, Lord, how can I thank you?"

"I have loved you with an everlasting love. I am the lover of your soul. You were meant to be with me for eternity, and now you shall be."

Then Jesus put one hand on Vicki's shoulder and the other atop her head. "I pray that from my Father's glorious, unlimited resources he will give you mighty inner strength through his Holy Spirit. And I pray that I will be more and more at home in your heart as you trust in me. May your roots go deep into the soil of God's marvelous love. And may you have the power to understand, as all God's people should, how wide, how long, how high, and how deep his love really is. May you experience my love, though it is so great you will never fully understand it. Then you will be filled with the fullness of life and power that comes from God.

"Now glory be to God! By his mighty power at work within us, he is able to accomplish infinitely more than we would ever dare to ask or hope. May he be given glory in the church and in me forever and ever though endless ages. Amen."

FIFTEEN

Carpathia's Demise

IT HAD happened so quickly, Vicki thought. And for everyone—a million people had experienced a personal encounter with Jesus.

Vicki moved back to her place and took Judd's hand. He and Lionel worshiped God in silence and with tears. But no one seemed ashamed of the emotion. They were all in the presence of the one who had loved them enough to die for them.

The next few minutes were a blur as Vicki thought of her encounter with Jesus. The Lord spoke, praying to God the Father for the people.

Gabriel also spoke finally, saying, "The Lord is faithful; he will make you strong and guard you from the evil one."

At the mention of the evil one, the archangel Michael brought forth Nicolae

Carpathia, Leon Fortunato, and the three Carpathia look-alikes—Ashtaroth, Baal, and Cankerworm—Vicki had seen on video a few months earlier. These were demonic creatures bent on deceiving the nations.

Gabriel leaned down to the three and said, "As a fulfillment of age-old scriptural prophecy, you kneel this day before Jesus the Christ, the Son of the living God, who, though he was God, did not demand and cling to his rights as God. He made himself nothing; he took the humble position of a slave and appeared in human form.

"And in human form he obediently humbled himself even further by dying a criminal's death on a cross."

"Yes!" the three squealed. "Yes! We know! We know!" And they bowed their deformed bodies.

Gabriel continued: "Because of this, God raised him up to the heights of heaven and gave him a name that is above every other name, so that at the name of Jesus every knee will bow, in heaven and on earth and under the earth, and every tongue will confess that Jesus Christ is Lord, to the glory of God the Father."

"Jesus Christ is Lord!" they hissed. "Jesus Christ is Lord! It is true! True! We acknowledge it! We acknowledge him!"

Jesus leaned forward. " 'As surely as I live,' says the Sovereign Lord, 'I take no pleasure in the death of wicked people. I only want them to turn from their wicked ways so they can live.' "

"We repent! We will turn! We will turn! We worship you, O Jesus, Son of God. You are Lord!"

"But for you it is too late," Jesus said with sorrow in his voice. "You were once angelic beings, in heaven with God. Yet you were cast down because of your own prideful decisions. Rather than resist the evil one, you chose to serve him."

"We were wrong! Wrong! We acknowledge you as Lord!"

"Like my Father, with whom I am one, I take no pleasure in the death of wicked people, but that is justice, and that is your sentence."

The three look-alikes screamed in pain, their snakelike bodies shedding their clothes. Then they burst into flames and were finally carried away by the wind.

Now it was Leon's turn. He wailed and sobbed, casting away his robe and shoes. "Oh, my Lord and my God! I have been so blind, so wrong, so wicked!"

"Do you know who I am?" Jesus said. "Who I truly am?"

"Yes! Yes! I have always known, Lord! You are the Messiah, the Son of the living God!"

"You would blaspheme by quoting my servant Simon, whom I blessed," Jesus said, "because my Father in heaven revealed this to him? He did not learn this from any human being."

"No, Lord! Your Father revealed it to me too!"

"I tell you the truth, woe to you for not making that discovery while there was yet time. Rather, you rejected me and my Father's plan for the world. You pitted your will against mine and became the False Prophet, committing the greatest sin known under heaven: rejecting me as the only way to God the Father and spending seven years deceiving the world."

"Jesus is Lord! Jesus is Lord! Don't kill me! I beg you! Please!"

"Death is too good for you. How many souls are separated from me forever because of you and the words that came from your mouth?"

"I'm sorry! Forgive me! I renounce all the works of Satan and Antichrist! I pledge my allegiance to you!"

"You are sentenced to eternity in the lake of fire."

"Oh, God, no!"

"Silence!" Gabriel said, and Leon crawled away sobbing.

Vicki had prayed for Leon's and Nicolae's demise, but she couldn't help feeling sorry for both of them. They had defied God and persecuted his people. Now they would pay.

Michael grabbed the elbow of a defiant Carpathia and spun him around. "Kneel before your Lord!"

Carpathia sneered and wrenched away from Michael.

Jesus said, "Lucifer, leave this man!"

With that, the air seemed to go out of Nicolae. His hands and fingers became bony. He looked like a helium-filled balloon a week after the party, all shriveled and shrunken. When Gabriel ordered him to kneel, the potentate got on all fours.

As Nicolae lowered his head, Jesus said, "You became a willing tool of the devil himself. You were a rebel against the things of God and his kingdom. You caused more suffering than anyone in the history of the world. God bestowed upon you gifts of intelligence, beauty, wisdom, and personality, and you had the opportunity to make the most of these in the face of the most pivotal events in the annals of creation.

"Yet you used every gift for personal gain.

You led millions to worship you and your father, Satan. You were the cunning destroyer of my followers and accomplished more to damn the souls of men and women than anyone else in your time.

"Ultimately your plans and your regime have failed. And now, who do you say that I am?"

Silence. Then a weak voice said, "You *are* the Christ, the Son of the living God, who died for the sins of the world and rose again the third day as the Scriptures predicted."

"And what does that say about you and what you made of your life?"

"I confess that my life was a waste," Nicolae whispered. "Worthless. A mistake. I rebelled against the God of the universe, whom I now know loved me."

With sadness Jesus said, "You are responsible for the fate of billions. You and your False Prophet, with whom you shed the blood of the innocents—my followers, the prophets, and my servants who believed in me—shall be cast alive into the lake of fire."

Gabriel stepped forward and said, "Then I saw the beast gathering the kings of the earth and their armies in order to fight against the one sitting on the horse and his army.

"And the beast was captured, and with him the false prophet who did mighty miracles on behalf of the beast—miracles that deceived all who had accepted the mark of the beast and who worshiped his statue.

"Both the beast and his false prophet were thrown alive into the lake of fire that burns with sulfur."

When Gabriel moved, a hole a yard in diameter opened in the ground, and a stinky smell burst forth. Flames erupted from the hole, and the crowd backed away. Michael walked Nicolae and Leon forward. Leon cried like a baby and tried to get away, but Michael pushed him into the fire, his cries fading as he fell. Then Michael pushed Nicolae in, and the man's screams echoed throughout Jerusalem. The hole closed, and the Beast and the False Prophet were gone.

Gabriel addressed the people. "Jesus is the true light, who gives light to everyone. But although the world was made through him, the world didn't recognize him when he came. Even in his own land and among his own people, he was not accepted. But to all who believed him and accepted him, he gave the right to become children of God. They are reborn! This is not a physical birth resulting from human passion or plan—this rebirth comes from God.

"So the Word became human and lived here

on earth among us. He was full of unfailing love and faithfulness. And we have seen his glory, the glory of the only Son of the Father. Amen."

Vicki hugged Judd and thought about all they had seen and heard. That Nicolae and Leon were gone was a relief, but what about Satan himself?

The answer came a few minutes later when Gabriel said, "But now you belong to Christ Jesus. Though you once were far away from God, now you have been brought near to him because of the blood of Christ. For Christ himself has made peace, and he has brought this Good News of peace to you Gentiles who were far away from him, and to you Jews who were near. Now all of you, both Jews and Gentiles, may come to the Father through the same Holy Spirit because of what Christ has done for you.

"So now you Gentiles are no longer strangers and foreigners. You are citizens along with all of God's holy people. You are members of God's family. You are his house, built on the foundation of the apostles and the prophets. And the cornerstone is Jesus Christ himself. You who believe are carefully joined together, becoming a holy temple for the Lord. Through him you Gentiles are also joined together as part of this dwelling where God lives by his Spirit.

"Since you have been raised to new life with Christ, set your sights on the realities of heaven, where Christ sits at God's right hand in the place of honor and power.

"Let heaven fill your thoughts. Do not think only about things down here on earth. For you died when Christ died, and your real life is hidden with Christ in God. And when Christ, who is your real life, is revealed to the whole world, you will share in all his glory.

"Be careful! Watch out for attacks from the Devil, your great enemy. He prowls around like a roaring lion, looking for some victim to devour. Take a firm stand against him, and be strong in your faith. Remember that Christians all over the world are going through the same kind of suffering you are. In his kindness God called you to his eternal glory by means of Jesus Christ. After you have suffered a little while, he will restore, support, and strengthen you, and he will place you on a firm foundation. All power is his forever and ever. Amen."

The crowd shouted "Amen!" and the multitude began worshiping and singing as Gabriel shouted, "Then I saw an angel come down from heaven with the key to the bottomless pit and a heavy chain in his hand."

The crowd cheered.

"He seized the dragon—that old serpent, the Devil, Satan—and bound him in chains for a thousand years."

People screamed, their hands raised.

"The angel threw him into the bottomless pit, which he then shut and locked so Satan could not deceive the nations anymore until the thousand years were finished."

Now the people seemed to quiet, then gasped in fear as the archangel Michael came forward with an enormous lion. Gabriel quieted them by saying, "But you belong to God, my dear children. You have already won your fight with these false prophets, because the Spirit who lives in you is greater than the spirit who lives in the world."

The lion's roar shook the buildings around them. Vicki dipped her head and clamped her hands over her ears. When she looked again, the lion had transformed into a giant snake and coiled himself around Michael's arms and legs. Michael wrestled it to the ground, but then it turned into a dragonlike monster. Michael pulled a heavy chain from thin air and subdued the flame-snorting creature.

Finally, the dragon calmed and became an angel brighter than any behind Jesus. The chain slid to the ground in a pile, and the being argued with Michael.

Jesus took control and said, "Kneel at my feet."

"I will do no such thing!" Lucifer hissed.

"Kneel."

Lucifer hunched his shoulders but knelt.

"I have fought against you from shortly after your creation," Jesus said.

"My *creation!* I was no more created than you! And who are you to have *anything* against *me?!*"

"You shall be silent."

It looked like Lucifer tried to stand and speak, but he could do neither.

Jesus continued, "For all your lies about having evolved, you are a created being."

The creature shook his head.

"Only God has the power to create, and you were our creation. You were in Eden, the garden of God, before it was a paradise for Adam and Eve. You were there as an exalted servant when Eden was a beautiful rock garden."

Jesus gave Satan's history as the being writhed silently. "You have opposed my Father and me from before the creation of man. A third of the angels in heaven and most of the population of the earth followed your model of rebellion and pride. This will earn for them and for you separation from almighty God in the everlasting fire prepared for you and your angels."

Jesus accused Lucifer of deceiving Eve, putting murder into Cain's heart, causing the suffering of mankind, blinding the minds of millions who did not believe in the gospel, and many more sins.

When Jesus finished detailing Satan's crimes, Lucifer gasped through clenched teeth, unable to speak.

Gabriel leaned over the angel of light and shouted, "Acknowledge Jesus as Lord!"

Satan clenched his fists and shook his head.

Jesus looked left where another hole opened and black smoke billowed. Michael moved to Satan with the chain. Satan fought him as a dragon, then a snake, and finally a lion. Michael struggled to chain the animal, picked him up under one arm, and flew into the smoky hole.

The crowd cheered but quieted when Jesus raised a hand. "Glory and honor to God forever and ever. He is the eternal King, the unseen one who never dies; he alone is God. Just as sin ruled over all people and brought them to death, now God's wonderful kindness rules instead, giving you right standing with God and resulting in eternal life though Jesus Christ your Lord. I stand before you this day as the King of Israel, he who comes in the name of the Lord."

From the clouds came praises and singing. Then Michael flew out of the hole holding a key. Satan and the chain were gone.

Jesus led his horse to the Temple Mount, where Vicki knew he would take his place on King David's throne. The crowds slowly scattered, many of them going back to their homes.

Vicki took Lionel's hand in one hand and Judd's in the other, and they walked through the streets, now filled with green plants and trees. It was a brand-new world.

SIXTEEN

Reunion

JUDD and Vicki took Lionel to Jamal and
Lina's apartment and were surprised to find
them preparing a huge meal. The two had
escaped the Unity Army and had hidden near
the Siloam Pool. They had fresh fruit, vegetables, and meat from a nearby market.

When they prayed for the meal, thanking
God, Jesus answered. In fact, each time Judd
spoke with the Lord, he spoke to Judd
personally.

Their talk over the meal centered on Jesus
and how his presence had changed things.
Wild animals seemed tame and walked
through the streets without attacking other
animals. And the fruits and vegetables were
said to ripen on the vine right in front of
those who picked it.

Lina and Jamal said they couldn't wait to

see their children who had died, but they understood it might be some time before that happened.

"Why's that?" Lionel said.

"You know how there was a gap between the Rapture and the beginning of the Tribulation?" Vicki said, taking a bite of steak. "It's the same with the Glorious Appearing and the beginning of the Millennium."

"How do you figure that?" Judd said.

"It's in Daniel's prophecy," Vicki said. "Something like seventy-five days. I can show you after dinner."

Jamal and Lina seemed impressed with Vicki's knowledge and wanted to know more. Vicki explained what she knew of prophecies from Daniel 12 and Ezekiel 40.

"So you're saying this seventy-five days is preparation time for Jesus?" Jamal said.

"Yes, at least that's what Tsion Ben-Judah taught," Vicki said.

"It only took six days for God to create the world," Lionel said. "Think of what this world is going to look like after seventy-five."

"So much has been destroyed through the judgments," Vicki said. "Tsion said God wants the earth to be like it was back in the Garden of Eden."

The conversation turned to when they would see those who had died during the

Tribulation, and Lionel raised a hand. "I've been studying this one. From what Tsion wrote and what I read in the Scriptures, we'll be seeing people like your kids—" he nodded to Jamal and Lina—"at the same time the Old Testament saints are resurrected. Old Testament people like Moses and David and Daniel will rule with Christ during the next one thousand years along with martyrs who died during the Tribulation."

"What about Christians who died before the Rapture?" Lina said.

"They were resurrected at the time of the Rapture," Lionel said. "They were part of the heavenly army behind Jesus."

Vicki looked away. "Which means my mom and dad were there. It all seems so unbelievable, and yet we saw it today."

"But my son and daughter, Kasim and Nada, they will be resurrected when?" Jamal said.

"Soon," Lionel said.

Conrad was so curious about what had happened to Global Community workers that he drove to a GC police station a few miles from Enoch's house. What he saw amazed him. All employees of Carpathia had died—presumably at the time Jesus spoke. Enoch taught that all unbelievers still alive would die soon.

Conrad, Shelly, and other members of the Young Trib Force had decided they would head toward Mount Prospect rather than toward Chicago with Enoch, but that changed when Enoch stood before the young people. He had just returned from a drive through Chicago.

"I know you've heard Jesus' voice just like I have," Enoch began. "I've been asking him what we should do, especially since prophecy seems to ignore America. I thought we might try to rebuild this as a Christian nation, but the Lord made it clear he wants us with him."

"What did he say?" Darrion said.

"He said, 'Fear not, Enoch, for you have rightly deduced that you and your flock are to be with me.' He said he would transport us, that we shouldn't be worried."

"When?" Janie said.

"That's what I asked." Enoch chuckled. "And Jesus said, 'Enoch, if God cares so wonderfully for flowers that are here today and gone tomorrow, won't he more surely care for you? You have so little faith! So don't worry about having enough food or drink or clothing. Your heavenly Father already knows all your needs, and he will give you all you need from day to day. So don't worry about tomorrow."

Enoch's eyes twinkled. "So we're going to Israel. I don't know how. I don't know exactly when, but I do know God is going to make a way."

When Vicki awoke the next morning one thought sprung to her mind. She was to go to the Valley of Jehoshaphat—the one created when Jesus set foot on the Mount of Olives. She nudged Judd awake and they dressed.

"I don't think we—"

"—should eat," Judd finished. "We should just go right to the valley. That's what the Lord seems to be saying to me too."

Jamal, Lina, and Lionel felt the same way.

Incredible, Vicki thought. *Jesus is speaking to us, leading us, and showing us exactly what to do. And he's doing it for everyone!*

Conrad and Shelly had taken a walk with Phoenix and now sat on a stone bench in the courtyard of the nearby mall. They had talked about Jesus the whole day, and when they weren't talking about him, they were talking with him or he was talking to them.

Shelly held Phoenix on her lap, scratching under his collar. The dog's eyes closed with contentment, and Shelly leaned over to Conrad. "He's asleep now. You can kiss me if you'd like."

Conrad smiled. Since Jesus had come, everyone had worked together, and no one argued or squabbled over petty things. He and Shelly had discussed their problems and worked things out, but now there seemed to be a new depth to their love.

Conrad leaned forward, closed his eyes, and kissed Shelly. When he opened his eyes, he saw that things were different. Instead of sitting on a stone bench in Palos Hills, Illinois, they were sitting on the sand in Israel in some kind of valley. And there were millions of people passing by them. Phoenix, still on Shelly's lap, opened his eyes, wagged his tail, and leaped to the ground.

The sky above filled with angels and the heavenly army. Conrad shielded his eyes—the light was so intense.

"Do you believe this?" Shelly gasped.

Conrad shook his head and smiled. "That was a great kiss."

They both laughed and stood.

Then the voice of Jesus spoke to Conrad's

heart, and from the look on Shelly's face, he was speaking to her too. "Conrad, when you see my throne, join those on my right, your left."

"Okay, Lord," Conrad said.

Jesus sat upon a throne on a platform before all the people. The sight of millions of people moving to the left and the right of Jesus made Lionel gasp. When Jesus told Lionel where to go, he obeyed and moved toward a smaller group. Most were headed to Jesus' left, and people there looked frightened.

"Worship the King of kings and Lord of lords!" Gabriel shouted, and everyone fell to their knees.

"Jesus Christ is Lord!" Lionel said along with millions of others.

Gabriel motioned for everyone to stand. "John the revelator wrote: 'I saw under the altar the souls of all who had been martyred for the word of God and for being faithful in their witness.

" 'They called loudly to the Lord and said, "O Sovereign Lord, holy and true, how long will it be before you judge the people who belong to this world for what they have done to us? When will you avenge our blood against these people?"

" 'Then a white robe was given to each of them. And they were told to rest a little longer until the full number of the servants of Jesus had been martyred.'

"People of the earth, hearken your ears to me! The time has been accomplished to avenge the blood of the martyrs against those living on the earth! For the Son of Man has come in the glory of his Father with his angels, and he will now reward each according to his works! As it is written, ' "At that time, when I restore the prosperity of Judah and Jerusalem," says the Lord, "I will gather the armies of the world into the valley of Jehoshaphat. There I will judge them for harming my people, for scattering my inheritance among the nations, and for dividing up my land.

" '"They cast lots to decide which of my people would be their slaves. They traded young boys for prostitutes and little girls for enough wine to get drunk." ' "

A commotion rose from Jesus' left, and the group fell down and wailed, "Jesus Christ is Lord! Jesus Christ is Lord!" A man dressed in black with long hair tried to stand. *Z-Van!*

Calmly, the Lord spoke. "Lionel, come, you who are blessed by my Father, inherit the Kingdom prepared for you from the foundation of the world. For I was hungry, and you fed me. I was thirsty, and you gave me a drink. I was a stranger, and you invited me into your home. I was naked, and you gave me clothing. I was sick, and you cared for me. I was in prison, and you visited me."

"Lord, when did I see you hungry and feed you or thirsty and give you something to drink?" Lionel said. "Or see you as a stranger or see you in prison?"

"I assure you, Lionel," Jesus said, "when you did it to one of the least of these my brothers and sisters, you were doing it to me!"

Lionel nodded. "Thank you."

Jesus walked to the edge of the platform. With emotion in his voice he said, "Away with you, you cursed ones, into the eternal fire prepared for the Devil and his demons! For I was hungry, and you didn't feed me. I was thirsty, and you didn't give me anything to drink. I was a stranger, and you didn't invite me into your home. I was naked, and you gave me no clothing. I was sick and in prison, and you didn't visit me."

Millions protested. "When did we see you hungry or thirsty or a stranger or naked . . . ?" The noise of their pleadings reached a crescendo.

Then Jesus said, "I assure you, when you

refused to help the least of these my brothers and sisters, you were refusing to help me. And you will go away into eternal punishment, but the righteous will go into eternal life."

After a time, Gabriel stepped forward and silenced the crowd. "Your time has come!"

Jesus lifted a hand, and a huge hole opened in the earth to his left and swallowed the millions who had never received Jesus as their Savior and Lord. Then the earth closed again.

Vicki was overcome with sadness at the destruction of the people. Jesus spoke to her softly. "I know your heart, Vicki. Now accept my peace. The peace I give isn't like the peace the world gives. So don't be troubled or afraid. Listen now as my servant comforts you."

For the next few minutes, Gabriel spoke, giving Scripture, explaining the unexplainable—the love of God, the grace of Christ. Jesus spoke as well, and after Gabriel told everyone to sit, he smiled and said in a loud voice, "Blessed and holy are those who share in the first resurrection. For them the second death holds no power, but they will be priests of God and of Christ and will reign with him a thousand years.

"The mighty God, the Lord, has spoken; he has summoned all humanity from east to west! From Mount Zion, the perfection of beauty, God shines in glorious radiance. Our God approaches with the noise of thunder. Fire devours everything in his way, and a great storm rages around him. Heaven and earth will be his witnesses as he judges his people.

Jesus stood. "Bring my faithful people to me—those who made a covenant with me by giving sacrifices."

From everywhere came the souls of those who had died in faith, the "believing dead," as Tsion had called them. All these wore clean, white robes and gathered around Jesus' throne. Vicki searched the faces for anyone she knew, but there were so many!

Jesus began by honoring Old Testament saints, people Vicki had heard about when she was small and went to vacation Bible school. As Jesus called them forward, he embraced them and they knelt at his feet. "Well done, good and faithful servant," Jesus said to each.

Noah, Samuel, Ruth, Gideon, and many more approached Jesus. The ceremony must have gone on for days, Vicki realized, but Jesus had given everyone his strength and patience.

When Abraham stepped forward, Jesus said, "By faith you obeyed when God called you to leave home and go to another land that God would give you as your inheritance. You went without knowing where you were going. And even when you reached the land God promised you, you lived there by faith— for you were like a foreigner, living in a tent. And so did Isaac and Jacob, to whom God gave the same promise. You did this because you were confidently looking forward to a city with eternal foundations, a city designed and built by God."

Abraham's wife, Sarah, was right behind him and later Jacob and Joseph. Vicki was thrilled at the sight, but her heart ached to see her friends, those who had died during the Tribulation and those who had been taken from her in the Rapture.

She took Judd's hand and squeezed it gently. "Can't wait to meet your parents," she whispered.

SEVENTEEN

A New Family

THE honoring of Old Testament saints was complete, and Judd couldn't believe it had been days since it had first begun. He didn't feel tired, hungry, or anything other than worshipful toward Jesus. He thanked God again and again for letting him be a part of this.

"You're welcome, Judd," Jesus said. "But the best is yet to come."

Judd had dreamed of talking with Old Testament heroes, but now Gabriel stood and said, "John the revelator wrote, 'I saw the souls of those who had not worshiped the beast or his statue, nor accepted his mark on their forehead or their hands. They came to life again, and they reigned with Christ for a thousand years.'"

This ceremony didn't happen like the Old

Testament saints. Somehow the Lord arranged it so that only people who knew a Tribulation saint saw that person getting their reward. One of the first Judd noticed was Bruce Barnes, the pastor who had helped him, Vicki, and Lionel understand the truth.

Vicki stood and pointed at a white-robed man. "It's Bruce!" Before Judd or Vicki could yell at him, Mark Eisman stepped forward. Tears streamed down Judd's face as Mark received his reward. Then came Mark's cousin John Preston. Then Perryn Madeleine, the young man who had been beheaded in France. Then Pete Davidson, the biker Judd had helped during the earthquake.

Vicki wept as Natalie Bishop knelt in front of Jesus. The Lord honored her by mentioning that she had sacrificed her own life to save her friends. Natalie had worked inside the Global Community and had been eventually beheaded.

Vicki could hardly contain her joy as Chaya Stein and her mother stepped forward. Mr. Stein was not far away from Vicki. He stood, praising God, tears streaming.

Hattie Durham appeared and embraced Jesus. When she knelt at his feet, Jesus placed a sparkling tiara on her head. "My daughter, you were martyred for your testimony of me in the face of the Antichrist and the False Prophet, and so you will bear this crown for eternity. Well done, good and faithful servant."

Phoenix barked when Ryan Daley, an original Young Trib Force member, approached. The dog ran up to Ryan and licked his face. Ryan knelt at Jesus' feet. As Jesus gathered Ryan into his arms, the Lord reached out and gently patted Phoenix's head.

When Vicki looked again, Ryan had moved away, and Chloe Williams took his place. Behind her were Buck Williams and Tsion Ben-Judah. Caleb, the angel who had appeared to Vicki and the others in Wisconsin, stepped from behind the throne and embraced Chloe.

Jesus said to Chloe, "You too suffered the guillotine for my name's sake, speaking boldly for me to the end. Wear this crown for eternity."

To Buck, Jesus said, "You and your wife gave up a son for my sake, but he shall be returned to you, and you shall be recompensed a hundredfold. You will enjoy the love of the children of others during the millennial kingdom."

When Tsion Ben-Judah stepped forward,

Jesus praised him for "your bold worldwide proclamation of me as the Messiah your people had for so long sought, the loss of your family—which shall be restored to you—your faithful preaching of my gospel to millions around the world, and your defense of Jerusalem until the moment of your death. Untold millions joined me in the kingdom because of your witness to the end."

Lionel set out to find Ryan Daley as soon as he saw him approach Jesus. He jumped up and tried to see over the throng, but suddenly the honoring of these martyrs and saints was over.

Jesus stood at the front edge of the platform and spread his arms. "I will declare the decree. The Lord has said to me, 'You are my Son. Today I have become your Father. Only ask, and I will give you the nations as your inheritance, the ends of the earth as your possession. You will break them with an iron rod and smash them like clay pots.'

"Now then, you kings, act wisely! Be warned, you rulers of the earth! Serve the Lord with reverent fear, and rejoice with trembling. Submit to God's royal Son, or he will become angry, and you will be destroyed in the midst of your pursuits—for his anger can flare up in an instant. But what joy for all who find protection in him!

"I welcome you, one and all, to the kingdom I have prepared for you. Lionel, welcome."

"I praise you, Lord," Lionel said.

And then the noise of reunions began. People swarmed through the crowd looking for anyone to hug. Some grabbed strangers and embraced. Others who found friends or relatives leaped into the air, hugging each other tightly.

Someone touched Lionel on the shoulder and he turned. A familiar face looked back at him, and for a moment Lionel didn't know who it was. Finally he recognized the man and shouted, "Uncle André!"

Lionel's uncle smiled and turned his head shyly. "Bet you didn't expect to see me here."

"B-b-but . . . Judd and I . . . we found your body," Lionel stammered. "What happened?"

"All that stuff you said—I took it to heart. Just before I died, I cried out to the Lord to save me, and he did. I'm glad you never gave up on me."

Judd fell to his knees as Bruce Barnes and Ryan Daley walked arm in arm toward him and Vicki. Phoenix trailed not far behind, his tail wagging and his body trembling with delight. In the background, Judd saw Dan and Nina Ben-Judah embracing their father and Mrs. Ben-Judah close by.

Ryan knelt and hugged Judd. Then Vicki joined them, and they laughed and cried at the same time.

The joy Judd felt was so real he couldn't stop crying. He shook his head. "Ryan, I'm so sorry for—"

"No!" Ryan exclaimed. "There is no sorrow here. You've been forgiven. I've been forgiven. We've all received God's grace."

Bruce Barnes joined the little group. "We've been so proud of what you've done. There are many souls here because of your faithfulness to give the message."

"It's because of you that we even found the message," Judd said to Bruce.

Bruce nodded and his eyes widened. "Excuse me. I see my wife and children."

Lionel pulled his uncle André into the group and introduced everyone. When Ryan saw Lionel, Judd thought Ryan would jump out of his skin. They hugged and danced and slapped high fives.

Judd turned and looked toward the throne. Jesus watched, drinking in the excitement and fervor of the reunions. "Thank you," Judd whispered.

"You're welcome, Judd," Jesus said. "I delight in giving you the desires of your heart." He looked slightly to his left. "There are others who wish to greet you."

Judd turned and saw his mother, father, brother, and sister. Beside them were people he had never seen before. He rushed to his mom and hugged her, then his dad.

"I was on a plane—I took a credit card—," Judd started but couldn't finish.

"It's okay, Son," his father said, hugging him tightly.

Marc and Marcie beamed at Judd, then looked at Vicki. "Are you his wife?"

"Yes," Judd said. "Let me introduce you."

But before he could, Vicki let out a squeal.

Vicki flew to her mother and father and embraced them. Then she hugged her little sister, Jeanni, and twirled her around. "Mom, Dad, I want you to meet Judd Thompson."

Mrs. Byrne smiled. "Thank you for watching out for our little girl."

Judd dipped his head. "She's the joy of my life." He looked at Mr. Byrne. "If I could have, I would have asked your permission before we were married."

"You have our blessing and our thanks," Mr. Byrne said. "I couldn't have picked a better son-in-law."

Vicki quickly introduced her family to Judd's, and it felt like they had known each other all their lives.

Later Vicki found Pete Davidson and Natalie Bishop, and she had a chance to talk more with Ryan Daley. She saw Darrion Stahley walking with her mother and father. Manny Aguilara and his sister, Anita. Josey Fogarty with her sons, Ben and Brad, and people she had known in high school who had disappeared.

Chad Harris, the young man Vicki had met in Iowa, smiled and gave her a hug. Judd and Chad talked for a long time. Vicki spotted Cheryl Tifanne visiting her son, Ryan Victor, and spoke with her about her last months in Wisconsin. Vicki met Tom and Luke Gowin, two believers from South Carolina who had lost their lives. Judd seemed overjoyed to introduce a handsome young man named Pavel Rudja to Vicki. She later learned that Pavel had been in a wheelchair for most of his life.

As families headed toward homes and living quarters, Judd talked about their future.

He mentioned Vicki's idea about taking in children with no families.

Vicki stopped, noticing several children standing alone. A light caught her eye and she glanced at Jesus.

"Let the little children come to me," Jesus said. "Don't stop them. For the Kingdom of heaven belongs to such as these."

"Am I supposed to—?"

"I have already put this desire in your heart, Vicki," Jesus said.

Vicki walked up to a redheaded girl who was moving a finger through the sand. She couldn't have been older than seven.

"What's your name?" Vicki asked.

"Anne," the girl said.

"Where's your family?"

"I don't have any. They're gone."

Vicki looked at Judd and extended a hand to the girl. The three walked toward a boy sitting on a rock, and Vicki smiled at Anne.

"You have a family now," Vicki said.

In that day the wolf and the lamb will live together; the leopard and the goat will be at peace. Calves and yearlings will be safe among lions, and a little child will lead them all.

ISAIAH 11:6

ABOUT THE AUTHORS

Jerry B. Jenkins (www.jerryjenkins.com) is the writer
of the Left Behind series. He owns the Jerry B. Jenkins
Christian Writers Guild, an organization dedicated to
mentoring aspiring authors. Former vice president for
publishing for the Moody Bible Institute of Chicago,
he also served many years as editor of *Moody* magazine
and is now Moody's writer-at-large.

His writing has appeared in publications as varied
as *Reader's Digest*, *Parade*, *Guideposts*, in-flight maga-
zines, and dozens of other periodicals. Jenkins's
biographies include books with Billy Graham, Hank
Aaron, Bill Gaither, Luis Palau, Walter Payton, Orel
Hershiser, and Nolan Ryan, among many others. His
books appear regularly on the *New York Times*, *USA
Today*, *Wall Street Journal*, and *Publishers Weekly*
best-seller lists.

Jerry is also the writer of the nationally syndicated
sports story comic strip *Gil Thorp*, distributed to news-
papers across the United States by Tribune Media Services.

Jerry and his wife, Dianna, live in Colorado and
have three grown sons.

Dr. Tim LaHaye (www.timlahaye.com), who conceived the idea of fictionalizing an account of the Rapture and the Tribulation, is a noted author, minister, and nationally recognized speaker on Bible prophecy. He is the founder of both Tim LaHaye Ministries and The PreTrib Research Center. He also recently cofounded the Tim LaHaye School of Prophecy at Liberty University. Presently Dr. LaHaye speaks at many of the major Bible prophecy conferences in the U.S. and Canada, where his current prophecy books are very popular.

Dr. LaHaye holds a doctor of ministry degree from Western Theological Seminary and a doctor of literature degree from Liberty University. For twenty-five years he pastored one of the nation's outstanding churches in San Diego, which grew to three locations. It was during that time that he founded two accredited Christian high schools, a Christian school system of ten schools, and Christian Heritage College.

Dr. LaHaye has written over forty books that have been published in more than thirty languages. He has written books on a wide variety of subjects, such as family life, temperaments, and Bible prophecy. His current fiction works, the Left Behind series, written with Jerry B. Jenkins, continue to appear on the bestseller lists of the Christian Booksellers Association, *Publishers Weekly, Wall Street Journal, USA Today*, and the *New York Times*.

He is the father of four grown children and grandfather of nine. Snow skiing, waterskiing, motorcycling, golfing, vacationing with family, and jogging are among his leisure activities.

Hooked on the exciting
Left Behind: The Kids series?
Then you'll love the dramatic audios!

Listen as the characters come to life in this theatrical
audio that makes the saga of those left behind
even more exciting.

High-tech sound effects, original music,
and professional actors will have you
on the edge of your seat.

Experience the heart-stopping action and suspense of the end times for yourself!

Five exciting volumes available on CD or cassette.

CONFIDENTIAL	
Take a look at the confidential files of a new series, Red Rock Mysteries, by Jerry Jenkins and Chris Fabry . . .	
* * * * *	COMING MAY 2005

He didn't want to kill them. He just wanted the evidence back. If they made it to the police with the picture, he was dead. Back in jail.

If only those annoying kids hadn't forced this. Twins. A boy and a girl. And their little brother and dad. Now they would all have to pay.

He could see the fright in the kids' eyes as he pulled beside their Land Cruiser. The girl held a cell phone to her ear.

He rammed his car into theirs and sent them swerving. The dad got the Cruiser under control and sped up.

He matched their speed and pulled beside them as they approached a lake. This was it. He would take care of the problem right here. He swerved and forced them off the road.

The Land Cruiser hit a patch of snowy grass. Taillights flashed, but it was too late. The car flew into the air and plunged into the lake. As water engulfed the car, it slowly rolled over like a sunning sea lion, then sank with its spinning wheels pointing up.

He slowed to watch frigid bubbles rise. No one could survive this. Some mother would cry tonight.

He clicked his radio as he drove away. "The situation's under control."

The Future Is Clear

Check out the exciting Left Behind: The Kids series

Discover the latest about the Left Behind series and complete line of products a

www.leftbehind.com